Home This Christmas

BOOKS BY SUE ROBERTS

SUE ROBERTS

Home This Christmas

bookouture

Published by Bookouture in 2025

An imprint of Storyfire Ltd.
Carmelite House
50 Victoria Embankment
London EC4Y 0DZ

www.bookouture.com

The authorised representative in the EEA is Hachette Ireland
8 Castlecourt Centre
Dublin 15 D15 XTP3
Ireland
(email: info@hbgi.ie)

ISBN: 978-1-80550-064-3
eBook ISBN: 978-1-80550-065-0

PROLOGUE

I feel the biggest tingle of excitement as I anticipate my evening ahead at the new Riverside restaurant.

Autumn into Christmas is always one of the best times for Guy Haynes, the hot new name in the culinary world who has invited a string of his celebrity friends to the opening of his latest restaurant. I am happy to be one of the food reviewers going along.

'What time will you be back?' my boyfriend, Ade, asks as he lounges on our huge Italian leather sofa. It was thrilling being able to afford some stylish home furnishings when I began to earn some serious money.

'Not sure. There is bound to be a real buzz with it being opening night.'

There is a rumour that the new Superman actor might be in attendance, as he is apparently a friend of Guy.

'Okay,' he says, with half an eye on the old episode of *Top Gear* he is watching.

'I did ask if you wanted to join me,' I remind him. I fasten some silver earrings into my ears, before applying a slash of dark red lipstick in front of the stylish lounge mirror. I've gone for a black jumpsuit this evening, the same colour as my long, curly hair. I would really have loved Ade to accompany me to the restaurant, but I guess there will be other times.

'I know you did. My work buddy is in a bad way after his breakup, as I told you. He's coming over for a pint and a take-away later,' says Ade, switching off the television. 'Anyway, I'm sure there will be more of these restaurant evenings.'

'Of course there will.' I walk over and gave him a quick kiss. 'Lots more hopefully.'

Truthfully, though, I get the impression Ade can't be bothered coming out with me to these events lately. I know they are not really his thing – and most of the time, I review restaurants alone – but there is always a plus-one invite for opening nights.

He confessed only the other day that he was a little tired of visiting fancy places, surrounded by people he didn't know. He admitted to occasionally longing for the days when we would grab some fish and chips on the way home from our local pub when we lived in our previous, some might say, grotty flat on the wrong side of the river.

When my career took off, suddenly I was no longer Ruby Holmes, working for a local newspaper and living in a cramped flat, but food critic and darling of *Britain's Best Cook*. I was shot into the stratosphere and Ade came along for the ride.

Don't get me wrong, I enjoyed our life back in our old place too, but we move on, don't we? I'd always known it would not be forever, as I was determined to make a success of my career. It's what I moved to London for after all.

Our current home is on the third floor of a sleek glass and steel high-rise apartment with views of the Shard. By day, the flat is bathed in natural light and by the glow of the city lights in the evening.

I am not sure my mum thought I had it in me, to move from the Yorkshire village where I was raised and make it in the city. She would roll her eyes and tell me I was a dreamer whenever I talked about the restaurant-lined London streets and the opportunities they might offer. I sometimes wonder if her lack of faith had spurred me on to do well.

'If you fancy joining me later, get a cab down. There's usually always a good after-party on an opening night,' I tell him cheerfully.

'Might do. Let's see,' he says noncommittally.

I head out to the taxi and try not to dwell on whether Ade will appear later. Instead, I distract myself with thinking about who might be there tonight. There have been rumours that one or two members of the royal family would be in attendance, along with the owner of a Spanish restaurant that has several Michelin stars. Sometimes I have to pinch myself, that this is my life.

There's a queue as we pull up, extending out under the Christmas lights already up along the street. A pap shouts at a well-known supermodel who duly poses for a shot after emerging from a blacked-out car.

Another food critic steps out of a taxi then, her frosty expression fixed on the door as we make our way inside. She once told me that she loves to see the fearful look on restaurant staff whenever she enters a building, which I find baffling. I guess some people just love the power.

I grab a complimentary glass of champagne from the waiting staff carrying trays of filled flutes and take in the space. The decor is stunning; shimmering gold foil lights hang from a wooden ceiling, and the lights from the city are pouring in through the floor-length windows.

I swivel round to see Ged, a critic I really like, dressed smartly in jeans, shirt and velvet jacket combo. He has floppy red hair and always has the biggest grin. I have always liked Ged; he's fair in his critique, if a little over generous at times.

'How are things?' I ask my fellow food critic who writes for a magazine.

'Good, good. Probably eating too much, but then what would you expect in this line of work?' He laughs as he pats his slightly rotund stomach. 'Especially at this time of year. I've been eating bloody mince pies since October. It's my guilty pleasure.' He winks.

'I know what you mean.' I laugh. 'I wish they wouldn't put them in the shops so early.'

'So where is Ade off to tonight, then?' asks Ged as he sips his drink.

'Oh nowhere. He's having one of his friends around, who is having a bit of a personal crisis.'

'Oh right.' He frowns briefly before smiling once more.

'Anything wrong?' I ask him.

'What? Oh no, nothing. I thought I saw him earlier near a train station. Obviously, it wasn't him.' He shrugs.

Why would Ade have been heading out and to a train station? Maybe he had a change of plan – although it would have to have been very last minute. He was expecting his friend around within the hour. I am pretty sure it was just someone who looked like him...

'Was he alone?' I find myself asking.

'Erm, yeah definitely. If it was him, that is...' He smiles, a little uncertainly. 'It was dark after all, and I wasn't close enough to say hi.'

Guy Haynes welcomes us all then and gives a short speech before we are directed to our seats.

'Looking forward to this,' Ged says, rubbing his hands together.

'Me too!' I enthuse as I follow him to our table.

The food is utterly brilliant. My favourite dish is dessert as always: a sweet and warming ginger-infused cheesecake, which is fitting for the season. We are entertained throughout the evening by a rather wonderful singer and pianist – and a table of well-known comedians, who are seated on the next table, keep us all giggling with their wisecracks. The party goes on quite late in the end, with everyone clearly having the time of their life celebrating Guy and his new baby.

We say our goodnights, and as I travel home in my Uber, I push down a feeling of disappointment that Ade never showed up. I had texted him at some point in the evening asking if his friend had left, and if he fancied coming over, but he never read the message. I can't help thinking about why Ged thought he saw him near the tube station this evening.

London is always busy before Christmas – it took a lot of getting used to when I first moved. But Ged knows Ade pretty well. He wouldn't have mistaken him for someone else, surely? But if it was Ade, I wonder where on Earth he could have been heading?

ONE

The next morning, I am determined to enjoy our breakfast, rather than dwelling on Ged seeing Ade at the station. When I tiptoed in during the early hours, Ade was home, in bed fast asleep.

We are sitting in our kitchen, eating breakfast, a bacon sandwich on thick sourdough bread, and chatting about some of my up-and-coming jobs. We have nothing planned for the rest of the weekend, so it will be nice to relax. Maybe we will take a walk to a park later and have an evening watching a new series on Netflix.

'I'm looking forward to next Friday; it should be fun,' I say to Ade as I sip my delicious coffee, dispensed from our shiny coffee machine.

'Yeah, hopefully!'

'Although I do feel a little nervous.'

'Nervous?' Ade looks puzzled as he places his coffee cup down. 'What is there to be nervous about?'

I remind him of the celebrity cook-off for Children in Need, that will be televised live to the nation. Two other well-known presenters and I will be competing against each other. I am excited to have been invited to do this, although a little apprehensive too. I feel far more comfortable critiquing other people's dishes.

'Because this time it will be other people judging us. I'm hoping my go-to lamb curry will hit the spot.' I laugh. 'But I might just have to practise it one more time.'

'Did you say next Friday?' Ade asks, frowning slightly.

'Yes. I did talk to you about it,' I say breezily. In fact, I have mentioned it several times, as I feel both excited and nervous.

It is the first time I have been asked to do something for Children in Need and hopefully, it will lead to some more television work. Much as I love being involved in *Britain's Best Cook*, I am keen to take on other work. My dream job would to be a presenter on a travel programme, showcasing and sampling regional dishes around the UK. Maybe even Europe.

'I lose count these days,' says Ade. 'There are so many events. Next Friday, though, really?' He shakes his head as he pushes his plate away.

'I know, that has come around quickly, hasn't it?' I say excitedly. But he doesn't answer. 'Is everything okay?' I ask, picking up on his lack of enthusiasm.

'No, not really,' he says, looking me in the eye. 'As you seem to have forgotten it's my dad's seventieth birthday party next Friday. I thought that's what you were looking forward to. I wondered why you said you were feeling nervous.'

'But your dad's birthday is at the end of the month, isn't it?' I ask, confused.

Surely, I could not have got that wrong? I quickly bring up the calendar on my phone.

'It is, but the party is for this weekend. It's in the diary,' he says, stone-faced.

The only event in my calendar for next Friday is the Children in Need evening. Ade's dad's birthday is highlighted one week later, on his actual birthday. My heart sinks.

'Are you sure you told me the party was this coming Friday?' I ask, feeling dreadful that I could have got it so wrong.

'Yup. I told you before I booked the restaurant that I could only get the whole family together the week before. But as it isn't a foodie review, you probably weren't paying attention. I mean, you could have reviewed the restaurant if you liked, to see if it met your standards.' His jaw tightens.

'Ade, I'm so sorry, it's a genuine oversight,' I tell him, feeling truly awful. I like Ade's father a lot. How could I have not put the correct date in my diary?

'So, can you cancel the Children in Need thing?' Ade asks.

I wait a second too long before I respond. 'It's live television, Ade; you know I can't do that.'

'Thought not,' Ade says, avoiding eye contact.

'Ade, be reasonable I can't just pull out now, I—'

He places his plate and coffee cup into the dishwasher, before grabbing his coat from a stand near the front door.

'Where are you going?' I ask him.

'Out,' he snaps.

'Ade, can we at least talk about this?' I plead.

'Is there any point?' he says, turning to face me. 'Let's be honest, your work will always take priority over everything.' He quietly fumes. 'And don't get me wrong, that's fine most of the time. But the important stuff? I really thought you could at least show up for that.' He shakes his head.

'I would have, but as it isn't your dad's actual birthday, I truly forgot the party was taking place a week early.' I try to explain.

In fact, I can't even recall a conversation about it, despite Ade assuring me that we had discussed it. Was it something he casually dropped into a conversation? I feel bad that it isn't in my diary.

'Don't worry about it,' he says as he opens the door.

I don't have time to reply, as he slams the door behind him and leaves.

TWO

Two days later, I hold my breath as I hear the key turn in the front door.

I had chewed my friend Coleen's ear off, and drunk too much wine on the evening he left, and she had listened patiently as I went over and over the same things. She had tentatively mentioned that Ade and I hardly ever went out together these days, and maybe our relationship had hit a rocky patch. Perhaps she was right, and I just didn't want to face up to it.

'Hi...' I say. Ade looks tired and is sporting stubble on his chin.

'Alright,' he replies, barely able to meet my eyes.

It has only been a couple of days, yet in that time, I've already suspected things might be over between us. At least he texted me to tell me he was okay.

I have had sleepless nights, the thoughts going around in my head, wondering how we got here. Were things really so bad between us? I can't help wondering why Ade never discussed how he felt, but then he was never very good at that.

'Are you staying?' I ask, searching his eyes.

'I think we need to talk.'

My heart sinks as I face the inevitable.

I make us coffee, and we sit opposite each other, Ade on a chair, me on our sofa. I had imagined us falling into each other's arms, yet sitting here now, we seem a million miles away from that.

'I think we need a break.' He stares into his coffee cup. 'Paul from work has offered me his spare room,' he explains as his eyes finally meet mine. 'I think he is grateful for the rent since he split with his girlfriend.' He half smiles.

'Is that what you really want?' I ask him, my heart breaking, yet deep down realising he is probably right.

'Not exactly, but things are hardly working between us anymore, are they?' He sighs.

'Is this about your dad's birthday party?' I ask, although I know that one incident would not cause us to break up.

'Maybe it was the final reminder that we are on totally different paths...'

'How long have you felt this way?' I ask, feeling suddenly empty.

'For a while. I'm not sure who I am anymore...' he confesses. 'All of this—' He sweeps an arm around the room. 'Lovely as it is, it is hardly me, is it?' He raises an eyebrow. He had always been so content with our old flat and friendly neighbourhood.

'No, I don't suppose it is... The coffee machine is good, though, right?' I raise my cup and manage a smile whilst swallowing down a lump in my throat.

'I'm sorry, Rubes,' he says quietly. 'I think meeting Paul in our old local made me realise how much I missed my old life. It would be better if you came with me, but I know that isn't what you want. And who could blame you? You have worked hard for everything you have.'

'Was that the evening your friend was meant to come over here?' I ask.

'It was – sorry I never mentioned it.' He shrugs. 'We decided to go out in the end.'

So, Ged had been right about seeing him at the station after all.

We sit quietly nursing our coffees in silence, before Ade heads into the bedroom to collect his things.

'I am just nipping out,' I tell him, unable to bear the thought of a final parting.

'Take care, Ruby...' Ade says as he looks at me one final time. 'I'll leave my key on the dresser.'

'You take care too,' I tell him as I head out before he can see the tears in my eyes.

* * *

Ade was right, of course; we were on different paths. He was content with his lot, and craved a predictable, uncomplicated life that I had long outgrown.

I've never really missed our old neighbourhood, although at the time I had liked the sense of community: the smiles and the 'good mornings' each day from the neighbours on the short walk to the train station. And the café on the corner did a decent takeaway coffee at half the price of the well-known chains. It definitely had its merits.

But where I am now is like coming home. The view from the bedroom is something I don't think I will ever tire of. Sometimes I have to pinch myself to believe that I live here.

Each morning after waking up, I make a coffee and take it onto the balcony, which has a spectacular view of London Bridge, as well as the Shard. It is a world away from the small village where I was raised.

This was our home together, though; we had our routines, our shows we loved to watch and meals we would cook together. Breakups are just so final, aren't they? And sometimes it is the little things that you miss. Ultimately, though, I think breaking up was the best decision for both of us.

Luckily, my work keeps me so busy that I barely have time to think about Ade too much, an irony not lost on myself.

Even so, when my birthday rolled around a week later, I thought I might have heard from him, but there was just radio silence. I couldn't help feeling disappointed.

'What did you expect?' Coleen asked when we met for a coffee in a cosy café, its interior already strung with Christmas lights and a decorated tree in the corner.

'I don't know.' I sighed. 'I thought we could at least wish each other a happy birthday... We were together for over three years. What's wrong with still being friends?'

'Maybe, but I don't really see the point in maintaining any contact when a relationship is over.' She had shrugged. 'If it's over it's over. Best to move on.' Coleen is mistrusting of couples that remain friends after splitting, which I think is rather cynical.

Had I been selfish in our relationship, I now wonder? Food reviewing is my job and passion, which I thought Ade under-stood... It still hurts that he thought I would casually disregard his dad's birthday party. It had been a genuine oversight and I'd always liked his dad.

I put away the magazine I am reading in a stylish bamboo rack and get ready to head into the TV studios for a run-through of *Britain's Best Cook*. I realise I'm getting used to being on my own these days. I have friends and a wonderful job I adore. I remind myself that things could be a whole lot worse and to count my blessings whenever I am feeling down. When I return from work later, it will be dark, and I will by greeted by the magical view from my lounge windows of London in all its glory. I've worked so hard for everything in my lovely life. And right now, despite a feeling of slight sadness over the demise of my relationship with Ade I am not sure I would have it any other way.

THREE

I think I might actually be dying. It is two days before the Children in Need show, and I am lying in bed with my body refusing to move.

Even the hairs on my head ache, as I run my fingers through it. When I attempt to swallow down some water from a bottle on my bedside table, it's like sipping broken glass.

I manage to slowly drag myself to the kitchen for some more water and paracetamol, before I reach into a drawer for a thermometer. My temperature is through the roof. I am soon tucked back up in bed, my head pounding. This cannot be happening to me – I am almost never ill.

I somehow manage to phone my boss at the station; every word I speak is an effort.

'But you can't be ill; it's the final run-through for the show later,' she says in an almost clipped tone.

'I am ill. *Really* ill,' I croak. 'I don't think I will even be able to make the actual show the day after tomorrow.'

There is silence at the end of the phone.

'Hmm. Well, I guess I could ask your agent if Amanda Lewis is free,' my boss says eventually. 'She has been desperate

to break into TV for a while now – all she has had so far are
adverts, following her *Storytime for Kids* show. This could be
her big break.'

'Great,' I mutter, cursing this bad luck. I am NEVER ill. So
much for that echinacea and vitamin D I have been consuming
these past few months. I have a good mind to ask for a refund.

Amanda is actually really lovely, if a little over enthusiastic,
which probably comes from presenting kids' TV for years. I
kind of hope she isn't too good, though. I am aware of how
replaceable presenters are.

'Fine. Well, I only hope she is available at such short notice.
Let me know when you will be resuming work,' she says, and
then she is gone.

'Yes, I will get well soon, thanks for caring,' I mutter as I end
the call.

I text Coleen, feeling very sorry for myself, and she replies
with a GIF of a teddy surrounded by hearts, and a promise to
call in after work with some provisions.

I can't believe I am ill! I think of how quickly we can be
replaced in this business... but I push that thought away. I am
being paranoid. I have been a presenter for years after all. A few
salt gargles and a good night's sleep should hopefully see me
right. At least I hope so.

I would scream loudly if my throat allowed it. This really
cannot be happening.

'Oohh, you look rough.' Coleen sprays her hands with antibac
spay as she enters the apartment and keeps a respectable
distance.

'Cheers. I'm surprised you aren't wearing a mask,' I say as I
sip some iced water.

'I did consider it,' she says seriously. 'I am having my nieces
to sleep over for a couple of nights over Christmas and I cannot

afford to be ill. We have lots planned, including a trip to Winter Wonderland. Plus, I have a bridal fitting and two evening dresses to complete by the end of the week.'

Coleen is a dressmaker who makes such beautiful gowns and is always in demand, especially at specific times of the year. Prom dresses for school leavers are a big thing, as are ball gowns for black-tie events. More recently she's been getting requests for wedding dresses, which she has to carefully consider. She's reluctant to do bridal wear full time knowing she might one day encounter a Bridezilla.

She whips a paper mask from her bag and fastens it over her face. 'You can't be too careful. Winter viruses are so easily transmitted to other people,' she mumbles.

'Probably too late,' I tell her. 'You have already breathed in as you entered the germ zone.'

She heads to the kitchen area and begins to unpack a shopping bag onto the kitchen counter. 'Chicken soup will help with your cold. It's from the deli,' she informs me.

'It's not a cold, it's flu!' I protest.

'I also have some nice soft bread rolls,' she says, ignoring me. 'I thought sourdough would be a bit scratchy on your throat. Oh, and I bought some fresh ginger and honey. You have lemons, don't you?' she asks, before locating a mug. I point to the lemons in a wire fruit bowl on a shelf.

She sprays her hands with antibac once more before she flicks a kettle on, and soon enough I am presented with a delicious warming drink.

'You really are a pal,' I manage to croak, but my voice has all but disappeared now and I feel a little lightheaded.

I'm not sure what I would do without Coleen – she has come to my rescue so many times. In front of the camera, I appear to be the most self-assured, confident presenter out there, yet off screen I often have a crisis of confidence.

I mean sure, I am good at writing foodie reviews but there

are probably dozens of presenters who would kill for my job, having worked their way up in the industry and taken on several questionable roles in the process. Just like Amanda Lewis. My presenting job on *Britain's Best Cook* kind of fell into my lap after a slightly drunken chat when I was sitting next to the producer one evening at a wedding.

'Don't you think most people are handed an opportunity in life?' Coleen had reasoned when I had been doubting myself. 'Being given a chance is one thing; proving you can come up with the goods is another,' she told me firmly. 'My mum once got someone a job at her hair salon as a favour, but they didn't last five minutes.'

'Because they just couldn't cut it?' I had joked, and we roared with laughter. But that's the thing with Coleen, she always makes not just me, but everyone around her feel better. I often think that she would make a good counsellor.

'Anyway, you should make the most of being holed up here; it's crazy out there and it is only the first day of December,' she tells me now. 'I even came across some Christmas carollers.'

She shakes her head, and her silky blonde bob falls back into place as it always does. My curly hair has a mind of its own and takes time and lots of taming products before it looks the way it does. This morning it resembles a burst cushion and will have to stay that way – at least for the time being.

'Some people like to spread the cost of Christmas, though.' I remind Coleen of those who can't afford to go out all at once and grab a big haul of gifts.

There was a time when I would have been one of those people, picking up presents throughout the year, and taking advantage of sales.

'I suppose so.' She warms the soup in a microwave before pouring it into a bowl, along with a fresh bread roll.

'Oh, this smells delightful. Thank you, Coleen, I really do appreciate it,' I rasp.

'You're welcome. I am sure it will do you some good.' She glances at her watch. 'Right, I must dash. I'll call you later. Back to bed after your soup – I am sure there are a ton of Christmas films you can get your teeth into, now that it's December.' She winks.

'Sounds perfect,' I croak.

She air-kisses me from a safe distance, and I slowly manage to finish every drop of the delicious soup, before crawling back to my bed.

I still can't believe I'll miss the live TV show – but I can barely speak. Amanda as my replacement, though? I mean, I would never wish bad things on anyone, yet a part of me is hoping that she doesn't make *too* good a job of it. If she does, then who knows what might happen? Maybe I will be replaced by the ten-years-younger-than-me glamorous blonde. Great.

I flick the TV on, and find a suitably cheesy, happy-ever-after movie. If only real life were like that, I sigh to myself. The guy in the movie is impossibly handsome, not to mention a real gentleman, holding doors open and complimenting the main character at every opportunity.

I suppose psychologists would call it love bombing, given that they have only just met at a Christmas market and he has already bought her a coffee, told her she is beautiful and invited her to accompany him on an overnight stay to New York. I find myself hoping that alarm bells are ringing in her head. That is before I remind myself it's a movie, where everything is magical and improbable. I bet she doesn't come down with a stinking virus on their next date.

I watch the credits roll before snuggling down beneath my expensive feather duvet and allow myself to sleep once more. Sleep is the best medicine, I tell myself, hoping I'll feel better soon.

Drifting off, I think how differently we all deal with heart-break. I couldn't eat a thing and lost almost a stone in weight when my dad died over four years ago. My appetite has been a little off after Ade and I split too. Thankfully that form of grieving hasn't gone on for long – it would be inconvenient to say the least, in my line of work.

I was always close to my dad – and my mum once upon a time, but not so much these days. Not that she is a bad mum or anything, she's just hardly ever around since Dad passed away, seemingly wanting to fill her time with activities that take her off somewhere.

She is currently in Kenya volunteering at a game reserve. We keep in touch by emails and phone calls, though, and she sometimes sends me some cute videos of the animals. I reflect that it might be nice when she returns home in a couple of months to get some quality time together. Perhaps a spa break in a nice hotel or even a few days in the sun.

I shuffle to the kitchen to make myself a hot drink and then peek out of my curtains and glance out at the view that never fails to lift my spirits. An apartment block to the left has a Christmas tree in the window, the lights gently twinkling, reminding me that Christmas Day will be here before I know it.

Soon enough, I'll be offered free mulled wine and all manner of Christmas goodies at restaurants and cafés across town, in the hope I will endorse them in my weekly column. Last year I was gifted so many boxes of shortbread and panettone, I donated them to a local food bank.

Flicking through some photos on my phone, I come across several from two years ago at Christmas time with Ade. He had joined me at a pub in the city after I had just dined at a new Asian restaurant for a review. Sadly the restaurant has since closed. The restaurant business is so fickle and astronomical rent rates in the city centre don't help.

The photo shows us smiling and raising a glass, a roaring fire in the background, its surround decorated with a Christmas garland. It was exactly the type of pub Ade liked, and similar to the one in our old neighbourhood.

In some ways, it also made me think of the pub in the Yorkshire village I was brought up in. Everyone knew each other and there was often a celebration of one sort or another. Adults and children alike would have a wonderful time, and a bouncy castle would be erected in the outside area to keep the kids entertained.

Around this time of year the village had a tradition of all the children, me included, decorating the Christmas tree outside the church with handmade baubles and glittery snowflakes, our excitement infectious. There is a lot to be said for the simplicity in the village, and I can't help but smile when I think of Christmases gone by, when Dad was still here.

Sitting on my sofa and admiring the festive view with my hot drink, I check my phone for any messages, but there is nothing apart from the earlier one from Coleen.

I idly think about what would have happened, had I stayed in the village. Neighbours and local church people always rallied when someone was ill. Even with a bout of flu, someone would appear with homemade soup or a remedy sure to make you felt better, which would instantly lift your spirits.

I don't really have the energy to reply to my messages anyway, so it is just as well I don't have any. Time to finish my drink and catch up on a little more sleep. And pray my recovery is speedy.

FOUR

My voice vanished completely the following morning, but a few days later, I am fully recovered, and the TV station welcomed me back with open arms.

Amanda Lewis, although not exactly a disaster, never lit up the screen as the producers thought she might have done. I felt a little sorry for her as I watched her from my sick bed and she stumbled over some of her lines. It is daunting to be in front of a camera on something other than a kids' programme for the first time – although I imagine being a children's TV presenter is harder than it looks. Hopefully, the right opportunity will come her way in the future.

As I never normally get ill, I take it as a sign that I ought to look after myself a little more, starting with upping my exercise. Sure, I eat good food, but my hours can be irregular, which affects my sleep, and well, maybe I could cut back on the wine a little if I am honest. I decide that there is no time like the present so decide to head out for a walk.

Wrapping up warmly, I decide to take a walk along the river, before I nip into a gift shop I know along the way. Mum is due back in the new year, and I would like to buy her something special.

I breathe out the cold, crisp air. My dark hair is tucked beneath my woollen beret, and my long, quilted coat is keeping me toasty. The twinkling lights threaded through the trees I pass add pops of brightness to an overcast day.

I pass tourists dragging suitcases, chattering excitedly and stopping to take selfies outside of the Tate gallery, ready to embrace a break in the city. A mist hangs over the river as tourist boats stoically continue their trade, carrying passengers along the river at least until the darkness falls.

I peruse my favourite gift shop and buy my mum a pretty silk scarf and an unusual vintage silver ring that I know she will love. I contemplate buying myself a pair of soft, blue leather gloves before reminding myself I have several pairs at home. Not in blue, though. In the end, I talk myself into buying them.

After an hour, I stop at a café for a hot chocolate and a mince pie that I simply cannot resist at this time of year, and a woman, with a young lady I presume to be her daughter, recognises me.

'Excuse me, are you Ruby Holmes?' the older woman asks.

'Yes, that's me.' I smile, as I duly pose for a selfie with them, much to the delight of the mum.

We have a little chat, and I am suddenly reminded that I am a bit of a household name. At least to those who watch cookery shows. I get lots of smiles – which is not something generally considered a thing in London – when I walk around the city, so perhaps I am recognised more than I realise.

Walking past couples holding hands, or peering into shop windows, reminds me that I will be alone this Christmas, and although it doesn't exactly fill me with dread, I feel sad that things didn't work out with Ade. I feel so grateful having Coleen in my life, and my friend Sienna at the studio, who always cheers me up if I feel a little low.

Back home, feeling refreshed and energised, I find a cookery book that has a recipe for a Christmas cake that my mother used to make.

As I flick through the pages, I am transported to my childhood home and the smell of brandy as Mum would infuse the cake, in the run-up to Christmas. I recall her catching Dad having a sneaky shot of the brandy once and she scolded him sharply. At the time I thought it was a bit mean, but as I grew older, I realised she was simply concerned about his alcohol intake.

Our whole world fell apart after Dad died. He was a huge presence with his gregarious, some might say loud, personality that lit up a room and his kindness knew no bounds. The heart attack came on without warning at a Christmas party and his life had ended suddenly. Mum has hated Christmas ever since and often heads off to volunteer somewhere during the festive season.

Mum went through a period of anger towards my father following his death, insisting he could have avoided the heart attack if only he had paid a little more attention to his health. As an adult, I can understand her frustration, although I guess there was only so much she could have done. I grew up in a house thinking it normal to watch my father knock back whiskies in the afternoon, continuing on into the evening. He was loud and funny, but never appeared drunk, which I now realise was down to a high tolerance to alcohol.

Folding the cake mixture and inhaling the rich spices fills me with a mix of emotions, and as I place the cake in the oven and set a timer, the tears that I have held back since splitting with Ade flow freely. I cry for the end of our relationship, and I cry for my dad. I shed tears over Mum too, who I miss more than she might realise. Finally, I cry for myself, although I am not sure why exactly. I have everything I need and more, yet I suddenly feel sad and alone.

Later, when the cake is out of the oven, I head off to enjoy a luxuriously scented bath. Sinking into the soothing warm water, I begin to think that I'm not alone, that everyone has their down days at this time of year. But we have to believe that tomorrow will be a better day. One that I resolve to look forward to.

After last night's melancholy, I once more tell myself how fortunate I am. Christmas can dredge up mixed feelings of nostalgia and sadness for lots of people, many who are far worse off than me. I felt surprisingly light after shedding all those tears, and sinking into a scented bath, and feel ready to seize the day.

I am back in work for a run-through for *Britain's Best Cook*, when my work pal Sienna hands me an envelope.

'This came for you when you were off ill,' she says, passing me the handwritten letter. 'Old school.' She laughs. 'They probably want a signed photo.'

Most people contact the studio via email, but occasionally, a handwritten letter will arrive, usually from an older person, often as Sienna said, asking for a signed photograph.

I tear open the cream-coloured envelope.

'It's not too early to open these, is it?' Sienna asks, producing a huge tin of Quality Street. 'I found them in a cupboard in the kitchen.'

Sienna has a sweet tooth and is annoyingly one of those people that can eat whatever she likes without putting on an ounce of weight. Something to be envious of at this time of year, I would say.

'Are you sure they are not a gift for someone?' I ask cautiously.

'No, they are definitely for us lot; I saw the floor manager hide them in a cupboard under the sink. He complained that all our freebie booze and chocolates had gone before we even reached December.' She grins. Last year, one of the young lighting guys, fresh out of university, was found by a security guy as he was locking up, passed out and clutching an empty brandy bottle. 'So, he is obviously hiding the gifts, for now at least.'

'Not well enough, it would appear,' I say as she prises open the tin.

Having finally opened the letter, I slowly digest the handwritten words, as Sienna selects the chocolate in a purple wrapper. Suddenly, my past comes rushing back and I picture myself travelling on a train to London.

'Tell me to mind my own business, but is it anything interesting?' asks Sienna, unwrapping the chocolate and popping it into her mouth.

'Hmm,' I mutter, as I read the letter once more. 'It is definitely interesting.'

'So go on, then,' she says, rifling through the tin and glancing around the room like a child who is about to be caught red handed. 'Have you been left an inheritance from an elderly relative you knew nothing about?' she asks.

'Nothing nearly so exciting.' I smile at Sienna's overactive imagination. 'The administrator at the village hall of my old hometown in Yorkshire has invited me over there this Christmas.'

'What for?'

'They've asked me to judge the annual Christmas gingerbread-making competition.' My mind wanders back to previous years. 'I can't think why they have asked me to do that. I left the village when I was eighteen years old and I've not really been back since even to visit.'

'Duh. Because you are a well-known celebrity now,' she reminds me. I'm finally slowly beginning to recognise this, but sometimes I still forget.

My mum won the competition once, and was very proud as

I recall, although Dad had joked that he preferred her Christmas cake. Maybe it was because she had laced it with the brandy.

It all feels like such a long time ago, but it would appear the gingerbread competition is something that still takes place. I wonder if the village hall still looks the same, or whether it has had a refresh and been brought into the twenty-first century? Do village halls ever really change?

'It would be quite the coup having you there to judge the contest,' Sienna continues. She tosses the sweet wrapper in a bin, before rummaging around for another. 'I bet they don't get many celebrities in that neck of the woods.'

'Probably not,' I agree.

Brindleford village, though... I'm not sure how I feel – despite a vague feeling of curiosity – about rocking up to the place I left so long ago. On the other hand, I don't suppose it would do my image any harm, giving up my free time in that way. And someone did go to the trouble of sending a hand written note after all.

'I suppose it would be.' I smile, wishing Mum was around this Christmas – I could have taken her along with me. Maybe she would have liked to visit after all this time.

Mum moved away from the village following Dad's death, preferring to be in the bustle of Leeds and close to her sister, which I always thought was a mistake, as Mum had never been particularly close to my aunt. All her friends were in Brindleford, yet she was determined to leave them behind and move on with her life.

'So, will you go?' asks Sienna, and then immediately curses the corporate chocolate gifts due to her lack of self-control. I remind her that they were not exactly out on display, and she grins.

'I'm not sure,' I reply truthfully. 'Things are pretty full-on at this time of year for me.' But even to myself, it sounds like an excuse.

'It might be bad press if you don't go,' she suggests as she places the lid onto the tin of chocolates. She's not wrong. 'I mean, you don't want your old village to say that you have become too big for your boots, do you?'

'Do you think they might?'

'Possibly. They might say you are up your own backside, that sort of thing.'

'Gosh, I hope not,' I say, horrified.

'I'm joking!' She grins. 'Although they might think that...'

Would it matter to me if they did? It probably would, although I am not sure why. I think my mind is made up, though.

'And, you never know, you might actually enjoy it!' Sienna winks before heading off to put the box back in its rightful place in the cupboard.

Would I enjoy returning to the village I grew up in? There is no disputing that the villagers would go all out at Christmas, and I wonder if they still do? To this day, I don't think I have ever seen a more magnificent tree than the one that stands proudly outside the old church.

'Maybe I would...' I smile, although truthfully, I cannot imagine spending time in a place that holds so many memories, not all of them great. It's another world now.

But I suppose I can be there and back in no time. And after all, I do have a bit of a weakness for gingerbread.

FIVE

I was eighteen years old when I kissed goodbye to my first love, Nathan Woods, breaking both of our hearts in the process, but with a determined ambition to head down South.

Despite my parents worrying and preferring that I chose something up North, my heart was set on London. After leaving school, I had bussed to a college in a town several miles away and gained the qualifications to take me to university.

Nathan was born into a farming family and was helping with the day-to-day running of the dairy farm. He had no desire to head to the city, so we had no choice but to go our separate ways. At three years older than me, maybe he was ready to settle down.

'You will keep in touch, won't you?' Nathan had pleaded, his voice choking with emotion when we said our goodbyes at the train station. 'I want to hear all about London.' He forced a smile as he wished me well. I had offered him his ring back, but he shook his head and told me to keep it.

'Maybe you will think of me when you wear it,' he had said, trying to put on a brave face.

The train rumbled into the platform, me seconds away from

stepping onto it and heading for my new life. 'Course I will keep in touch,' I reassured him. That was when it felt real. I was moving away from Brindleford and saying goodbye to my first love. I did wonder if I was making the right choice, but the thought was fleeting. If I had stayed, I would have settled into a life that I knew I would grow tired of, however much it hurt to say goodbye to Nathan.

London had been a revelation, with its bustling streets and non-stop life, and thankfully, I loved it at once. I quickly settled into a flat share with three interesting people, one of them on the same course as me, the other two studying medicine and law respectively. It made for some interesting conversations when we would occasionally rustle up a meal and dine together.

I took part-time jobs waitressing and day by day, Nathan occupied less and less of my thoughts. I eventually graduated with a first-class media degree, and combined with my love of food, I managed to secure a job on a local rag. I wrote all about restaurants offering early-bird deals as they were called and gave my honest opinion of the food on offer.

In time, my old village became nothing more than a distant memory, even though I duly returned home for the first two Christmases, successfully managing to avoid Nathan, and risking opening old wounds. I managed to do so by spending most of the time holed up in the family home, watching movies, playing board games, and bypassing the local pub.

In my first year at university, Mum and Dad came to London for Christmas shopping and the 'bright lights'. She would tell me what Nathan had been up to and how she would often run into him, until I gently told her that maybe it was best not to know if I was to make a success of my life here.

They enjoyed their trip so much, it became an annual thing – until my dad passed away and Mum took to travelling alone. When she moved to Leeds to be close to her sister, there was no reason for me to head back to my childhood village.

Do I *really* want to revisit my past? I ask myself as I fold the letter and place it in my handbag. Would it be selfish of me if I don't go and judge the competition?

Having done a run-through of *Britain's Best Cook*, my mind slightly distracted by the letter, it isn't long before it's time to head home.

'Fancy a drink?' Sienna pipes up behind me as I grab my coat.

'I'm a bit done in.' I still feel a little tired after my recent bout of illness.

'No problem, rest up,' she says kindly.

One of the camera guys nearby agrees to go with her instead – that's how things are at the TV studio. A whole bunch of people who socialise here and there, but none of them are what you might really call close friends. I can't imagine calling any of them in the middle of the night, if I had a crisis, with the exception of Sienna.

Heading home on the tube, I pull the letter out of my bag and re-read it once more. I can't help but think of the life I left behind – especially my first love.

A group of slightly worse-for-wear Christmas revellers who are wearing Santa hats and sparkly tops board the train at the next stop, singing loudly. A man in a suit shakes his head – but what can you expect at this time of year, even though Christmas is still several weeks away? As they cling on to the overhead bar one of the women loses her grip and goes sliding along the carriage and stops at my feet.

'Oh fuck!' she mutters, her party hat askew, and her handbag two feet in front of her.

'Are you okay?' I ask, helping her to her feet and retrieving her bag and handing it to her.

'I'm okay.' She grins as her mate joins her. 'And cheers for that!' she says, gripping her bag for dear life. Her eyes focus on me as recognition dawns. 'Wait a minute, it's you! It is you, isn't it, you are off the telly,' she announces, and I feel several pairs of eyes turn to look at me.

I have my hat pulled over my head, hiding my trademark long curly hair, which normally means people don't recognise me, but it seems an inebriated woman can.

'Um, yes, I guess it's me.' I smile.

'Ah, well thanks for helping me,' she replies, slurring her words slightly. 'Wait till I tell my mum, although I don't think she likes you that much, 'cos my dad fancies you.' She giggles.

I can't help but feel flattered.

'Anyway. I don't think you would deliberately try and ruin the reputation of a restaurant,' she says drunkenly. 'No offence.'

'None taken – and I would never do that,' I say, feeling slightly stung by her remark.

At the next stop, the young woman and her group of friends depart the train and I watch her link arms with one of them as they make their way to the exit.

I stare straight ahead, avoiding eye contact with anyone and wonder why she said that about me. Was that just her opinion, or is that what the public really think?

Feeling a little hurt by her remark, I wonder if it is because I called out a dishonest restaurant owner for flogging cheap, bought-in food items and fleecing unsuspecting diners. I give an honest critique of the food I review, but it is always fair.

The review I gave a long time ago has resurfaced from time to time to haunt me. Maybe I *was* trying to make a name for myself at the time, although I felt justified in exposing the so-called quality establishment that was massively overcharging its customers and buying in sauces and desserts, that they passed off as home-made. Surely that could not have been a bad thing, me calling them out?

The restaurateur in question, taking zero responsibility for his actions, gave interviews to the tabloids the following year,

saying he was almost bankrupt and how I had been instru-
mental in ruining him.

I almost gave up the whole food reviewing at that point,
until my dad reminded me that the guy was ripping people off
and would probably have failed in the long run anyway. Plus,
the public seemed to be on my side too. The unscrupulous
restaurant owner faded into the distance before he came up
with the sob story for the press, obviously out to make some
money.

I dearly wish Dad was around to talk to. He always
managed to find the right words to say.

When I finally arrive home, I kick off my shoes and make
myself a coffee, which I take to a comfy armchair near the
window.

I sip my drink and glance out over the illuminated city,
feeling a little conflicted. Would the people from my childhood
village think I have become a little above myself if I refuse their
invitation? I wonder, pondering Sienna's comment. And why
would it bother me so much if they did?

Once more, my mind drifts to the village. I think of the giant
oak tree beside a footpath close to the church and how I fell to
the ground after climbing it with a group of children and grazed
the whole of my left thigh. My father scolded me and told me I
could have broken my leg, or worse. It was the only time in my
life I ever recall my father raising his voice to me, and I burst
into tears.

What exactly will I be doing here that would stop me from
going to Brindleford? Sure, there will be an evening out with
the studio crowd, and Coleen has invited me to spend
Christmas Day at her place, with her husband and in-laws, but
otherwise I don't have any real plans, aside from work. Truthfully, I kind of feel like holing myself up here this year on the
twenty-fifth, binging on Christmas food and too much televi-

sion. It has been an exhausting year, and I am looking forward to doing nothing for a few days.

Last year was so different. Me and Mum had spent the day with Ade and his family and had a wonderful time. I naively thought that we might spend the day together this year as we are both alone, but she clearly had other ideas. I hope she enjoys her Christmas, that will be very different this year.

My mind flits to the gingerbread competition that takes place at the same time every year, exactly one week before Christmas, at the village hall.

I suppose it would be a bit of a coup for the village to have a celebrity in attendance, and I can't deny that I am a little curious about who remains and whether any younger people have bought houses in the village. I also wonder how much it has changed over the years. Is the kindly vicar still there, who helped me up when I fell from the tree? And Marilyn who taught Sunday school at the church?

I guess there is only one way to find out, so before I head to bed, I fire up my laptop and reply to the invitation. It is time to revisit my past.

SIX

'But you will be back for Christmas Day, though, won't you?'

I am in town shopping with Coleen, taking a coffee break at a cute café near Covent Garden. The market has been transformed into a magical wonderland, the area strung with thousands of fairy lights and a towering Christmas tree dressed in red and gold. The cobbled streets are alive with shoppers, many of whom are taking a break in the café, laden down with bags, and sipping hot chocolates topped with whipped cream and marshmallows. The café is so warm I unwind my scarf and remove my coat, wishing I had not worn so many layers.

'Of course! I'll stay overnight as it's a bit of a trek, but yes, I will be back for Christmas Day.' I certainly don't want to be the sad person staying in a hotel and dining alone at Christmas, surrounded by groups of families and friends.

'I promise you will have a great day with us,' she says, squeezing my hand. 'I know it might be a bit strange without Ade, but it will take your mind off things, especially with my lot! Although my niece has a new karaoke machine so you might want to bring some earplugs.'

'Sounds fun. I might even treat you all to a rendition of my favourite Christmas song.'

'Maybe it's me that might need the earplugs,' she teases.

Coleen loves spending time with her two nieces, as she and her husband have no children, although it is not for the want of trying.

'Thanks, Coleen, I don't know what I would do without you.' I look gratefully at my best friend who has always been there for me. 'You really are the best friend I could ask for.'

I don't want to reject her invitation, and I know she means well, but I may have to see how I feel closer to the big day. Maybe I will want to feel the hug of a warm family, or perhaps I will prefer to dive into that new book I am looking forward to starting, alongside a cheeseboard and a decent bottle of red. It's good to know that I have options, though.

Outside, the contrast in temperature is so sharp, I'm glad of those layers after all as we walk, and my frosty breath hits the air. We take in the talented street entertainers, including a magician who has attracted quite a crowd. A child claps their hands and giggles wildly when the magic man produces a teddy bear from an empty hat, which he then hands to her.

'I don't suppose live rabbits would be allowed these days,' Coleen comments as we observe the sweet scene. 'Animal rights groups would never allow it.'

'Probably not,' I agree.

Further along, next to the impressive Christmas tree, a choir are singing such a perfect rendition of 'O Holy Night' that it almost brings a lump to my throat. It is all so joyfully festive, yet my heart still feels a little heavy as we walk.

This time last year, Ade had surprised me with a last-minute trip to a German Christmas market, and it was in between filming, so I was able to go. I'm not sure I would have done, if I'd been busy with work. Perhaps he had been right in saying our lives could never align. Deep down, was I happy to see where my career would take me, with or without him? It seems in life we will always have choices to make.

I tell myself not to get caught up with sentimentality, especially when we pass one of Ade's favourite gadget stores that we would spend hours in as he marvelled over the latest piece of wizardry.

'Shall we?' says Coleen, gesturing to a nearby stand selling mulled wine.

'Go on, then, as it's freezing.'

We stand sipping our delicious drink to the strains of a Christmas song being sung by a street busker nearby. A few people smile at me as they walk by, and one or two ask for selfies, which always amuses Coleen, and she tells me how proud she is to have a celebrity as a best friend.

'I don't feel like a celebrity.' I laugh as I fish into my pocket and throw a few pounds into the guitar case of the singer.

Our drinks finished, we go our separate ways as Coleen has arranged to meet a client with some material samples for a dress.

I head to the tube station, and as the doors of the train close with a hiss, a bloke comes haring down the stairs. As he draws closer to the train he has just missed, I can see that it is Ade. I stare at him from my window seat. We are literally several feet from each other, but our eyes do not meet. Should I wave? I am about to knock on the window, when Ade takes his phone from his pocket.

Is he about to call or text someone to tell them he will be late? I wonder, recalling the times we would do the same thing with each other. Surely it could not be a romantic interest, but then his departure was rather quick when I think about it. Perhaps he got chatting to someone in our old neighbourhood pub. I watch him pressing the phone to his ear and speaking into it. He could be calling anyone. I guess I will never know.

To my relief, I don't feel too bad after catching sight of Ade.

There was no sinking feeling in my heart, and as London is a big place, it's unlikely our paths will cross too much in the future, but if they do, I am sure it will be fine. Maybe understanding that we wanted different things has made the separation that tiny bit easier. Not for the first time in my life, I realise.

I take a deep breath and decide to look forward to my evening out with Coleen later at a stylish new bar. Suddenly I feel good about the future. I even dare to think that the best is yet to come.

Coleen and I spend a pleasant evening at the newly opened bar, where jazz music is playing in the background and I quickly get into the Christmas spirit over a few cocktails.

'Don't forget, you have an open invitation to Christmas lunch,' says Coleen. 'The first Christmas on your own is always tricky,' she says as she sips her drink through a straw.

'I know, and thanks,' I say, raising my glass to my friend and feeling touched by her thoughtfulness. 'Although, I think I will be just fine. I felt nothing but a little regret when I saw Ade today.' Once more, I realise my work has been my saving grace of late.

We say our goodbyes after a lovely evening, and it is almost midnight, when I receive a text from Mum telling me she will call me tomorrow, as it's probably a little too late to call now. I FaceTime her at once.

'Ruby, darling, how are you?' she asks brightly. She looks healthy, I notice, her skin lightly tanned, her grey hair swept up into a bun.

'Fine, Mum – and you? You're awake late, aren't you?' Kenya is three hours ahead of the UK.

'Oh, I am, but we have been taking it in turns to nurse an elephant calf. Abandoned after her mother had been killed by poachers.' She sighs. 'The cruelty of humans for the pursuit of money really does shock me sometimes.'

'Gosh. Mum, that's truly awful.'

'It is. The good news is, looks like she is going to make it.'

'Thank goodness,' I say, wondering what is wrong with some people in this world.

Mum once worked as a veterinary nurse at the village practice, so when the opportunity arose to help at the game reserve, she was off like a shot. Mum is in her late sixties, and I did worry about her initially, but it seems she has found a new lease of life.

'Sounds like you are really enjoying yourself, then?'

'It's been a wonderful experience: it's so beautiful here, and I am working with such a lovely bunch of people,' she gushes.

'That's nice, Mum.'

The selfish, some might say childish, side of me longs for her to say that she will get on a plane and head home to spend Christmas Day with me. Instead, she prefers to spend the festive season with a bunch of strangers and the thought of it has me swallowing down a lump in my throat.

'I will call you earlier one evening and show you the sunset!' she says as we are about to finish the call. 'It really is quite magnificent.'

'I will look forward to it. Night, Mum.'

'Goodnight, Ruby.'

Despite my disappointment at her not being here, I tell myself that I am a thirty-six-year-old woman, and a short time ago I was in a relationship. Even if I wasn't, Mum absolutely has the right to spend Christmas how she likes – though it stings a bit that she isn't here. I guess I just miss her.

I climb into bed exhausted after a long but pleasant day. Tomorrow I will be on the train journey up North and stay overnight at one of only two hostelries in my old village. Judging

the gingerbread contest in the village hall is the least I can do,
and you never know, I might even enjoy myself.

SEVEN

'Cancelled, really? It's only a bit of snow...' I say to no one in particular. I sigh in frustration as I view a board at the station informing me that my train has been cancelled due to bad weather.

'Aye, love. Everything stops in this country when there's a bit of snow.' The grey-haired man in a checked cap standing next to me shakes his head, as he goes on to tell me how he walked four miles to school in knee-high snow when he was a lad. 'Where are you off to then?'

'Brindleford. I was going to take the train to Burnley, then a connecting train to the village.' We both stare at the board, as if it might magically change and normal service will be announced.

'I was heading to Burnley too.' He rubs his chin with his hands. 'My son was going to collect me from the station.' He is quiet for a moment, seemingly deep in thought, before he speaks. 'Would tha be interested in driving up North with me?' he asks to my surprise, in his broad Yorkshire accent.

'Driving? But you are talking at least five hours, maybe more in this weather.'

'Hmm.' He nods. 'Ah well, maybe you will have to wait until tomorrow then, lass.'

I can't wait until tomorrow. The Christmas fayre is tomorrow. I wanted to arrive this afternoon, have dinner and an early night. I was hoping to judge the competition then head straight back to London. I guess I could just cry off given the train situation, but despite my initial reservation, something is almost pulling me there.

'So, are you going home?' I ask the older man.

'I'm visiting family. My son lives in a village in the countryside.'

'Right. Well, the train cancellation is certainly an inconvenience, but do you really want to drive there?' I ask him uncertainly.

'Why not? I've always been a good driver. Fifty years and only one accident, and even that was not my fault.'

I hope he hasn't just jinxed things.

I mull over his offer of a lift. It is only ten in the morning, so we could be there by late afternoon...

'Perhaps we could share the driving, if you are serious about it?' I suggest. 'In fact, I insist, it's the least I can do.'

'Aye, love, maybe we could.' He smiles. 'So, are we on, then? I am less than ten minutes away from here. We could get a cab and go and grab my car.'

The thought that the person I'm about to spend five hours in an enclosed space with could be a serial killer crosses my mind, but I reckon I am strong enough to fight off a bloke who looks to be pushing eighty. Besides, it might be nice to have someone accompany me on my journey. Before I can change my mind, I find myself agreeing to his proposition.

He calls his son then and explains the situation. He even hands the phone to me, and we have a brief chat. Perhaps he isn't going to murder me after all. And I realise it might be rather pleasant to chat with someone of a different generation. I used to love talking to my grandparents, who I often think of, especially around this time of year.

I insist on paying the cab fare from the station, and a short while later we pull up outside a block of council flats. The man, who has introduced himself as Henry, leads me to some garages at the rear, and soon enough we are driving his impeccably looked-after Vauxhall Vectra and heading for the motorway.

He fires up the radio and I quickly email the hotel to give them my new estimated time of arrival.

I can picture the Swan Inn, with its roaring log fire, and the huge Christmas tree that would stand in the entrance at this time of year. I recall the old-fashioned jukebox and shelves lined with books and board games, the landlord polishing the brass beer pumps until they gleamed, and his bubbly wife chatting away ten to the dozen to customers at the bar, and hope it hasn't changed too much.

I wonder whether the new owners have kept up the no-TV rule, encouraging conversations amongst the patrons? I hope so, although times have changed so much it seems unlikely.

'So, what brought you to London?' I ask Henry as we drive. The motorway is busy as always, but at least the weather is clear.

'You mean why did a Yorkshire lad like me defect to the South?'

'Well yes, something like that. It's very different down here.'

So different that since leaving, I've had no desire to head back to the tiny market town I come from. It feels so strange to be heading there now.

'Aye, it is, love. To be honest, I returned to London five years ago, although I was raised here as a young boy,' he discloses. 'I've all but lost my accent now,' he says, which I would highly dispute, but I don't say anything.

'What about yourself, then?' he asks, before telling me there are some mints in the glove compartment if I fancy one.

'I'm from a village not far from Skipton originally.'

'Are you?' He looks surprised. 'You have the most English accent I have heard. You could be one of the royal family.' He chuckles.

'Do you think so?' I laugh too.

I consciously erased my Yorkshire accent with elocution lessons, which probably does sound like I was trying to disguise my roots, but that wasn't necessarily the case. At the time, I thought it would secure me more work – even though there are lots of people with regional accents on television and radio these days. I explain this to Henry.

'Aye well, I reckon you should always be true to yourself. If people like you, they like you, if they don't, they don't,' he reasons.

Which is true about life in general I suppose. But trying to carve out a career in television, I thought I had better aim for a neutral accent. I don't think I sound like royalty, though. Do I? Surely my mother would have told me if I do.

We chat amiably and two hours later we stop for a drink at a café, just as the sky has turned a deep shade of grey.

Henry sips his tea and eats a toasted teacake that looks so good I order one myself.

'This is much nicer than those motorway services,' he pipes up about the café just off the M1 and I must agree.

The café with its laminated menus and home-cooked food feels warm and comforting. Christmas music is playing in the background and colourful, slightly gaudy foil decorations hang from the ceiling and every picture on the wall is framed with red tinsel. I feel as though I have stepped into a time machine back to the early nineteen eighties, if the old photos Mum has shown me are anything to go by. I find it rather comforting.

'Seems like we might get a bit of snow,' Henry muses, staring out of the window. 'I'd say that sky is full of it.'

'I hope not. At least not until we get to where we are going,' I reply, when a cheerful young waitress delivers my teacake.

'So, you're heading home for Christmas, then?' Henry asks as he sips his tea.

'Kind of.'

In between bites of the delicious, hot buttery teacake, I tell him all about being asked to judge the gingerbread competition in my old village hall and my work as a food critic.

'Well blow me down, I had no idea I was sitting here with a celebrity.'

He removes his checked cap and places it on the chair beside him and smooths down a few tufts of grey hair.

'I never think of myself as that,' I tell him truthfully. 'I just seem to have got lucky somewhere along the line.'

Why don't I eat more food like this? I'm almost tempted to lick my fingers.

'But I have always been honest in my reviews,' I continue. 'Which has not always gone down well.'

'Aye, well, some people don't like hearing the truth,' he says. 'But there is no such thing as luck when it comes to success. Hard graft is the key, although maybe a little bit of luck along the way, getting your foot in't door. But you must prove yourself in't long run,' he adds wisely.

'You're probably right.' I smile at this man I have known for little over a few hours, but I like him already. It pains my heart to know that I will never have the chance to enjoy little chats like this with my dad, who I miss so much, especially around this time of year.

Henry excuses himself for a minute, whilst he pops outside to call his son. I ask for another drink and settle the bill. I hand the waitress a ten-pound note, and her mouth gapes open.

'Thank you,' she says gratefully, as I wish her a merry Christmas. The tip was marginally larger than the bill itself, but

I remember the days working as a waitress on minimum wage when I was at university.

'All okay?' I ask when he returns.

'Aye, fine, love. I think my son Will is happy to know that I have a travelling companion.' He grins. 'He thinks I am a bit too old to be driving all this way.'

'Without being rude, perhaps he has a point...' I say kindly. 'I would be happy to take over the driving now, if you like?'

'If you like, love. Sometimes I have a little snooze around this time, so it is probably best.' He winks.

I smile back. 'In that case, it definitely is.'

Henry had told me during our chat in the café that he came to London to nurse his mother, who had lived in the big smoke since the nineteen-fifties after marrying a man she met whilst nursing. Unfortunately, Henry's father had died when he was a child, and his mother raised him as a single mother, so unsurprisingly, they were very close. Henry went back up North to study agriculture and met and married the love of his life, who passed away five years ago.

'It was funny really,' he recounted in the accent he thought had long disappeared. 'But it came at the right time to go and live with my mother in London and look after her. I was completely lost after Betty died.'

He told me he had enjoyed being back in London, with its bustling atmosphere that took him away from his own thoughts. 'So, I decided to stay. I help out on the community allotments. I have a lot of friends here now,' he explained.

'So you have no desire to return to Yorkshire, then?'

'Not now.' He shakes his head. 'I love the energy of London. I return regularly to see my son, though, and catch up with old friends,' he tells me. 'Those who are still of this world,' he says thoughtfully.

I grab a mint from the glove compartment before we set off, and as we continue our journey, Henry tells me his son is an architect and lives in a forest in an eco-friendly place, that he designed and built himself.

'Sounds amazing.' I imagine something sleek, made from glass and reclaimed wood.

'Aye, it's a smart place. A bit different from the flat in London, but I enjoy city life,' he says, answering what would have been my next question, as I wondered why he did not live closer to his son. 'Although it's nice to be in nature for a while, recharge the batteries – and I like the birds in the countryside.'

Half an hour later, Henry is gently snoozing to the sound of Christmas songs on the radio, and I sing along as I enjoy another mint humbug.

I am almost pleased the train was cancelled. Despite the long drive, I would never have got to know Henry. What a surprising start to the festive season, I think to myself as we turn off onto a slip road. Very surprising indeed.

EIGHT

'You made it!'

A tall, good-looking guy with fair, slightly curly hair pulls Henry into a bear hug as we get out the car, before shaking me warmly by the hand. He introduces himself as Will, Henry's son – though I've heard all about him from Henry on the way here.

'I can't thank you enough for this. Please, come inside and have a drink,' he suggests as he grabs his father's holdall.

I stand mesmerised by the exterior of the house, with its floor-to-ceiling windows that offer panoramic views of the surrounding countryside. I imagine the oak for the construction has been locally sourced.

Glancing at my watch and realising we have made good time without traffic, I accept the offer of a drink. I would love a nosey around the amazing-looking home.

'Maybe just a quick cup of tea would be nice,' I tell him, thinking of how much I enjoyed my Yorkshire tea earlier in the café. Maybe I will start drinking it again when I get back to London, rather than my usual latte. At least occasionally.

Inside, Will hangs his wax jacket on a hook in the front

porch, and we head into a cavernous room with high ceilings and a roaring log fire in the grate.

A tastefully decorated Christmas tree stands at the foot of a wooden staircase that leads to a mezzanine level, and the room is made cosy with rugs and well-placed art on the white walls. I don't think it would look out of place in a home interiors magazine.

'Right, what can I get you?' Will offers cheerfully. 'Coffee? Maybe a whisky?'

'Aye, lad. I'll have a whisky,' Henry replies as he rubs his hands in front of the cosy fire.

'Tea if you have it, and then I will order a taxi. My village isn't too far from here – I'm heading to Brindleford,' I tell Will.

'I know Brindleford, it's no more than a fifteen-minute drive from here – so you won't get a cab, I will drive you there,' he insists. 'It's the least I can do. Actually, you are just in time for dinner. I have had a casserole simmering on the stove all morning if you fancy joining us?' he offers.

'Oh no, really, I will grab something at the pub later. A cup of tea will be fine,' I say, even though the smell coming from the kitchen is very enticing.

'Ruby here is a food critic from the telly,' Henry tells his son.

'Really? Sorry I didn't recognise you; I don't watch much TV,' explains Will.

'I prefer it that way. It's refreshing for someone not to constantly ask me questions about the celebrities I've met. Or to feel nervous about serving me some food.' I laugh.

'Ruby here is judging the annual gingerbread competition in Brindleford,' Henry informs Will.

'Is that still a thing?' Will asks. 'I have never really got the hype around gingerbread.'

'The DIY gingerbread houses that are sold in the super-markets probably have a lot to do with it,' I say, thinking of how I might take one for Coleen's nieces if I pop over at Christmas.

'Maybe... And I am kind of relieved you are not eating here and giving my casserole marks out of ten,' he jokes. 'Please, take a seat; I will get that tea.'

As we sip our drinks, he asks me where I live, and I tell him all about my apartment in London.

'A bit different to here, then.' He glances out of the kitchen to the lush greenery surrounding the house. 'Although if you are anything like Dad, you will appreciate the peace and quiet.'

'I am sure I will. Although I am only here to judge the gingerbread competition, so I won't be staying long.'

'Sounds fun. I guess the organisers are proud to have you back in the village, now that you are a star.'

'Maybe,' I say, although truthfully it cannot be for any other reason. I would have been long forgotten by the villagers were it not for me popping up on their television screens.

'You have a beautiful home,' I compliment Will as I glance around. 'Henry tells me you are keen to build eco-friendly houses.'

'That's true. A lot of the materials used in this build are reclaimed or recycled. I guess I have always enjoyed recycling things, even as a child, hey, Dad? Although we never really called it that back then.'

'Oh aye, definitely. My garden shed was full of your junk, although I have to admit, you usually always made something from it,' Henry concedes. 'I remember you building a go-kart from some old pram wheels and planks of wood.'

'With your help.' Will looks affectionately at his father.

'Well, I had to supervise you. I once found him trying to launch a rocket he had made with some of my lighter fuel,' Henry tells me, and Will pulls a face.

'Gosh! So, you are an inventor too? I am impressed! Maybe

not for attempting to blow yourself up, though.' I giggle, and Henry roars with laughter.

'I am not quite so adventurous these days. For the last few years, I have concentrated on building projects, buying up land, and building affordable housing. There is a real demand for it in the area,' he tells me.

'Oh, I can imagine.' I think of the extortionate prices of property in London. I even know of one or two young people living in extensions in their parents' garden, as they try and save enough money for a house deposit.

'Well, your home is really beautiful,' I repeat.

'Thank you, that's very kind. As I said, it's a passion building sustainable housing as I think it is a good solution to the housing shortages, but not everyone agrees.'

'Why is that, do you think?'

'I guess they don't like the countryside being built upon... Don't get me wrong, I can see how it might upset someone to buy a house in a green area only to later have their uninterrupted views of nature obscured by new housing, but needs must...'

He offers me more tea, that I politely decline.

'I guess you have to build somewhere,' I muse.

'Exactly. And any available land is usually only in the countryside.'

Before I set off, I use the bathroom and it is every bit as stunning as the rest of the house, with a good mix of wood and stone, and a huge free-standing bath in the middle of the room. Apart from a dusky pink colour wall and towels, there are no female toiletries on display – unless they are neatly stored in a free-standing cupboard.

Downstairs, I shake Henry warmly by the hand, as I prepare to leave.

'Right,' says Will to his father. 'Help yourself to anything you need; I will be back before you know it.'

'No problem, the horse racing is just about to start.' Henry flicks on the television. 'And thank you again, love, it was a pleasure travelling with you.' He smiles at me warmly.

'The pleasure was all mine, and you helped me out too, remember. Merry Christmas, Henry.'

Will asks me a little more about my work as a food critic as he drives, which distracts me from the butterflies in my stomach about coming back after so long. Before I know it, we are pulling up outside the village of Brindleford.

Just then, the snow that has been threatening to fall begins to slowly drop from the sky. Huge snowflakes silently swirl onto the bonnet of Will's Land Rover as he pulls up at the end of the village high street.

'I won't hang about,' says Will, looking upwards. 'It was good to meet you, Ruby, and thanks again for travelling with Dad,' he says gratefully. 'Where are you staying?' he inquires as he climbs out of his seat and opens the door of the car for me. He then grabs my overnight case from the back seat and hands it to me.

'The Swan Inn,' I tell him, once more hoping that it hasn't changed too much. 'And it was a pleasure – thank you for the drink and the lift.'

As far as I recall, The Swan was the only pub with rooms in the village – the other pub being the Greyhound, a predominantly male drinking establishment that my mother used to call 'a spit and sawdust' type of place. I guess things must have changed a bit these days. Perhaps there are even a few Airbnbs in the area. As I take in my surroundings, I realise I had forgotten just how pretty it is around here.

'Right, well. Maybe I will see you again. Although perhaps not, if you are only here for one night. Anyway, good luck with the judging,' says Will cheerfully.

When he leaves, I find myself stood staring down the small high street and a flood of memories comes rushing back.

NINE

The metal sign of the Swan Inn, sandwiched between the general store and the butcher's shop, is gently blowing in the first flurry of snow. I pull my hood up and quicken my step, before the pavements turn slippery.

As I walk, I take in how things have changed over the years. I am surprised that the butcher's shop is still here, although it is obviously still used regularly by the locals. All those years back, I'd accompany Mum on a Saturday afternoon to buy a joint for the Sunday roast. Amongst the old – the grocery store and toy shop that have been here forever – there's also the new, including one or two coffee shops. I also spy a women's fashion shop that I may pop into if I get the chance.

And then I notice the village bakery and remember when Mum and I would stand staring at the tempting cakes before buying something to put in the fridge for after Sunday lunch. Custard tarts, meringues and chocolate eclairs were our particular favourites, and would always be placed in a white cardboard box and tied with string. I quickly realise that there will be memories here at every turn.

When I turned sixteen, the owner of the bakery offered me

a Saturday job, and I could hardly believe my luck. Especially when she taught me to bake, which is something I still do from time to time – particularly if I feel a little stressed. There is just something so soothing about folding a cake mixture or bringing together the dough for some delicious scones.

I take in an Italian restaurant that looks pretty, with white fairy lights draped across its window, and the word *Roberto's* emblazoned across the glass. It takes me a moment to realise that it is on the site of the once Greyhound pub that obviously is no more.

Across the road from high street and just off the market square stands the red-brick library, where I would spend hours completing my college assignments, before I headed off to university. The old church a little further along towers tall and proud as if watching over the village and keeping it from harm.

After a few minutes of taking in my surroundings, I am checked in at reception by a bubbly middle-aged lady.

The dark wooden reception desk that stands beside a staircase is comfortingly familiar. A stand on the desk is displaying leaflets about Christmas lunches in the restaurant and breakfast with Santa for the children. The thick, red patterned carpet and dark overhead beams, from which sprigs of holly are hanging, are offset by the cream walls.

'Welcome, love, looks like you got here just in time,' says the proprietor, noting the light dusting of snow on my coat and introducing herself as June. 'Hope you had a good journey?'

'I did, thanks.' I smile, not feeling the need to go into my last-minute change of plan. All I want to do is get to my room and unpack.

'That's good,' she responds warmly. 'Anyway, there is a welcome tray in your room, but if you need anything else, just give me a shout.'

'Thanks, I will.' Suddenly, I feel exhausted after the long drive and the unexpected tea stop.

She hands me an old-fashioned metal key attached to a wooden fob – so different to the electronic key cards I am used to in London hotels. 'Breakfast is between seven thirty and ten,' I am happy to hear. I sometimes wonder why people get up at the crack of dawn for breakfast, unless, of course, they have business to attend to.

'Oh and we have an open fire in the restaurant area,' she informs me as I am about to walk away. 'It's very cosy.'

'Sounds perfect.'

The separate restaurant area is something new, making good use of the cavernous space.

I can imagine sipping a drink in front of the open fire after a nice winter walk. I slightly regret not bringing a pair of walking boots, but then I wanted to travel light.

An olde-worlde room of more dark beams and a four-poster bed greets me as I push open the heavy wooden door. The huge bed has an inviting-looking, thick duvet with crisp white bedding, which I fling myself onto, after kicking off my boots and wiggling my toes with relief.

As I lie on the bed, taking in the cosy room, I can hardly believe I am actually here. I would probably be shopping in London now or enjoying some lunch with Coleen in a busy restaurant somewhere. I have to admit, though, I did rather enjoy getting to know Henry and being introduced to his undeniably attractive son. Maybe being here does have some advantages after all.

After unpacking, I make myself a hot chocolate, courtesy of the tea tray on a dressing table, and take it to a floral padded window seat that overlooks the high street.

As the daylight begins to fade, streetlights gently illuminate the road and the bulb lights that are strung across the road begin to gently glow. A string of gold foil angels playing trumpets are interspersed with red foil stars and stretch from one side of the street to the other, creating a pretty, festive scene.

I observe shoppers, laden down with bags, dashing along with hoods up as the snowfall continues. It is quite a different scene from my window back home, where the lights and buildings of the city spread out in front of me, although completely enchanting in its own way.

Sipping my drink, I take in the Dickensian windows of the toy shop across the road – it makes for a rather magical winter scene as the snowflakes fall to the ground. I immediately think of the excitement I felt as a child, when I ate the chocolates from my advent calendar as I looked forward to the big day.

One Christmas morning, I was presented with a wooden pink-and-grey-painted doll's house that I had admired in the toy shop window every time I walked past. I still have it packed away in a box in my spare room. I have wondered from time to time whether a thing of such beauty ought to be out on display somewhere, rather than locked away, despite me having no children of my own.

The snow settles on the rooftops and the pavement below, slowly turning everywhere into a winter wonderland. There seems to be no sign of it abating any time soon. I hug my drink and continue to enjoy the white view outside that is utterly charming.

I glance at Roberto's, once the site of the Greyhound, and close my eyes as I remember stumbling out of the pub one Saturday evening with Nathan. We had gone down a side alley and kissed passionately without a care in the world.

My life was so different back then; I barely recognise myself these days. I was happy, though, I think to myself as I rinse my cup and place it on the tea tray. At least for a while. But I was never meant to stay in Brindleford. I have no doubts about that.

It won't be long before I am back in London once more and as captivating as the view is outside, I can hardly wait.

As my thoughts turn to the competition tomorrow, a knot of tension appears in my stomach.

Is there a niggle of worry that Nathan will be there, along with the other villagers, but then again, why would he be? I can hardly see him entering a gingerbread competition, after all, but perhaps he will accompany a wife or girlfriend? And how will I react, if I do see him? Hopefully things would be cordial between us, with the passing of time. We both have very different lives now after all. In an ideal world, I'll be in and out of Brindleford without encountering too many ghosts from the past.

Deciding not to dwell on things, I google the number for the Italian restaurant across the road and luckily manage to make a reservation for dinner. If I am forced to stay here, I might as well have a nice meal – and Italian food is one of my favourites. It will be good to relax and not worry too much about tomorrow.

I choose a simple black pair of trousers and a red jumper with a hint of sparkle to wear this evening. As I make my way to the restaurant across the road, my coat tightly wrapped around me, I take in the quiet street with not a car or a person in sight, in contrast to the street outside my London home with its bright lights and busy traffic. At least the snow has stopped now, leaving everywhere looking like a scene from a Christmas card.

It's a little after eight, and the place is already half full, with the sound of gentle chatter around the room. I pass a large table of diners wearing party hats and sparkly Christmas outfits, and wonder if they are on a work night out. It smells divine, and a friendly waiter shows me to a table in the corner that overlooks the high street. The table is set with a chunky cream candle, wound with red tinsel at the base, giving it a festive touch. To the right, I have a view of the open kitchen, and my stomach gives a little rumble as I watch chefs sizzle and toss food in pans.

Glancing around, I feel as though I could be in Italy. One wall has a mural of the Trevi fountain; the remaining walls are painted a soft terracotta shade and adorned with black and white prints of various locations in Rome. There is soft lighting and 'That's Amore' is playing in the background.

My starter arrives and as I tuck in, I notice a couple of waiters glancing my way. Even the kitchen staff seem to be looking over, reminding me once more that I am someone that people recognise. Perhaps I ought to put them at ease and say I am not here to critique the food – but first, I have my starter to enjoy.

The aubergine parmigiana is delicious, and I am awaiting my main of ox-cheek pasta, when I hear someone say, 'Fancy meeting you here.' My heart stops. I steel myself as I look up, expecting to find Nathan standing in front of me, but it isn't him. Instead, it is Will, smiling broadly, and my heart rate returns to normal.

'I see you have discovered the best Italian restaurant around for miles – it's worth the drive over from my place, even in these conditions, I'd say.' He grins.

'Will! How nice to see you again; I didn't realise you had a reservation here this evening?' I say, feeling pleasantly surprised.

'Would you believe I burned the casserole' – he pulls a face – 'as Dad and I were so engrossed catching up. We ended up eating a sandwich.' He laughs.' 'This place is one of Dad's favourites, so we decided to head out. We're just leaving, actually.'

He gestures to a table, where Henry and a woman around Will's age are tucking their chairs in. The woman pulls on her coat, and gives a little wave, and Henry quickly comes over and says hi, before they depart.

'It's been good seeing you again.' Will smiles. 'Enjoy the rest of your time here.'

'Thank you. And safe journey home,' I add.

'Cheers.' I feel as if he is about to say something else, before he says goodbye for a second time and heads off.

I am too full for dessert, so opt for a liqueur coffee that really hits the spot. As I sip my drink, I wonder why I reacted the way I did, when I thought it might have been Nathan I encountered earlier?

'I hope everything was good?' An Italian-sounding man pulls me out of my thoughts, as he presents me with the bill.

'It was absolutely delicious. Really, it was wonderful.'

'Are you going to write about it?' he asks casually.

'Actually, I meant to tell you earlier that I am dining for pleasure rather than business this evening, but I was so absorbed with the food. But who knows? I may mention it in a column I write.'

A huge smile spreads across his face. '*Grazie*. I am Roberto, the owner,' he tells me proudly and shakes my hand firmly.

'Well, Roberto, you have a beautiful restaurant.' I glance around at the now packed-out room. 'I am not sure you need my review, as it would appear you are doing rather well already.'

'It is true, but after Christmas in the winter months, it's not so busy.' He shrugs. 'Maybe you could mention to your readers that we are open all year round. There are lots of good walking paths around here,' he points out.

'I will bear that in mind, Roberto. Thank you once more,' I tell him warmly. And he is right about the walking. There are footpaths into the stunning Yorkshire countryside all around.

I settle my bill, and as I reach the door, I can feel all eyes on me. Either it's just that people don't recognise me as being from the village, which can be the case in a small community, or they know me from the television... Or they are simply curious about a woman who is dining alone – something no one would bat an eyelid about in London.

Back at the inn, I quietly retreat to my room. Tonight, I don't have the energy for a chat with June, and bed is calling.

I think about bumping into Will this evening, and how he turned and glanced at me when he left the restaurant. I was so

sure he was about to ask me something before he disappeared...
I felt quite flattered when he turned to look at me, although also
a little surprised that he did it when he was in the company of
another woman.

In bed, I scroll through my phone for a few minutes. There
is a text message from Coleen, telling me she hopes all will go
well tomorrow and that she will call me when I'm home. I also
make some notes about the meal, thinking I genuinely could
mention Roberto's in one of my next columns. It really is one of
the nicest Italian restaurants I have been to in a long time and
deserves a recommendation. My eyes become heavy and start to
close as a bright idea starts to take shape. I could start featuring
places outside of London occasionally. Maybe I ought to
consider getting out of the city a little more and visit places I
would never usually consider. Broaden my horizons a little.

TEN

It takes me a second to remember where I am when I first wake, and I push down a slight feeling of nervousness.

I find myself thinking about Nathan, and wondering, not for the first time, if I have made the right decision coming here.

Downstairs in the breakfast room, 'Tomorrow' is being hummed by blonde-haired June as she bustles about. Occasionally she breaks into actual song, and I can't help but smile.

'Good morning, love.' She beams. 'Wishful thinking, eh, me singing about the sun coming out tomorrow.' She chuckles. 'It's as grey as a badger out there. There is nothing nicer than a crisp winter day with a blue sky, is there? I can't be doing with overcast skies,' she says with a grimace. 'Oh, by the way, the pavements have iced up overnight, so be careful out there. I was nearly doing my Jayne Torvill impression when I nipped out this morning.' She laughs. 'Right, love, full English, is it?'

I had been thinking about taking a walk after breakfast to the church to have a look at the nativity scene, so I'm grateful for her advice.

'Actually, I think I will just have some scrambled eggs, and coffee.' I'm still not really feeling hungry after last night's meal.

Besides, my stomach is turning over a little at the thought of judging the contest.

'Coming right up.' She winks as she bustles off humming a tune once more.

Great. It's now freezing and treacherous outside. I scroll through my phone and discover that trains are still disrupted, but normal service will be resumed either later today or tomorrow. Hopefully I won't end up stuck here after all.

It's not that I dislike being back in Brindleford. In fact, I am beginning to appreciate my old village and the small changes that have brought it up to date.

But... There's no denying that the main reason for me wanting to leave the village is so I don't have to bump into Nathan. I hate to admit it to myself, but I thought about him a lot when I was driving here. That's what we sometimes do when a relationship breaks down, though, isn't it? View a previous relationship through rose-tinted glasses, wondering what might have been. I don't regret anything, but all the same, I do not fancy running into him and possibly a wife.

'Thanks, June, that was delicious,' I tell her, as she begins to clear my plates away.

'We aim to please. Although I am disappointed you never went for the full English; the sausages from the butcher's next door are award winning.' She winks.

I may well have done myself a service not having a huge breakfast – I have been wanting to have a peek at the bakery... Maybe even sample something... 'Perhaps I will indulge another time,' I tell June.

'Well, it would be lovely to see you again, should you ever fancy a break from the hustle and bustle of London. That is assuming you won't be staying on for another night?' she queries.

'I suppose there is a possibility actually,' I tell her. 'The trains might be running as normal later today, but it seems unlikely.' I sigh. 'I keep checking my phone for updates on the situation in case things change.'

'Right you are. It's just that there have been one or two email enquiries about renting a room. So, if you are going to keep it for another day, I would need to know,' she says kindly.

'In that case, yes, I will have it for another night. You have a business to run after all.'

'Not a problem, hun. I will refresh your tea tray later, then.' And with that, she continues to bustle about.

I wind my blue cashmere scarf around my neck and pull on my heavy woollen coat and start to head over to the imposing eighteenth-century church, with its sandstone colour and beautiful stained-glass windows.

On the way, I pop my head into the bakery, and the scent of delicious vanilla hits my nostrils.

'Good morning.' A cheerful woman, her dark hair tied back in a ponytail, greets me with a wide smile.

'Morning,' I say, as I head towards the counter.

The bakery is painted in a pale yellow, with posters of cakes and Bournville chocolate on the wall, that give it an almost vintage feel, were it not for the modern lighting and sleek silver coffee machine behind the counter.

Beneath the glass counter are rows of giant pastries filled with cream in every colour of the rainbow, including what looks like buns with my favourite pistachio filling. Gone are the custard tarts and chocolate eclairs that I remember as a young woman.

'That is our best seller,' says the shop worker, as my eyes fall on a super-sized bun oozing with cream.

'It's raspberry and white chocolate. Although the pistachio is very popular, along with the salted caramel and chocolate tarts,' she informs me.

'Wow, everything looks divine!' I exclaim, as my eyes scan the treats in front of me.

'We do have the usual favourites such as vanilla slices that the older customers seem to love, but we sell out quickly in the morning.'

'I might just have to treat myself after I've popped into the church,' I say, glad I didn't go for the full English breakfast this morning.

'Here.' She pops a raspberry cream-filled bun into a paper bag with the name *Penny's* written across it. 'As it's the last one, it's on the house.' She winks.

'That's so kind, thank you.'

'I hear you are in town for the judging of the gingerbread contest,' she mentions cheerfully. I almost ask her how she knows who I am, before remembering I am a well-known face.

'I am.' I smile. 'And then I will be heading back to London for Christmas.'

'Rather you than me. About judging the contest, I mean, not going to London.' She laughs. 'It is so difficult to judge competitions, especially in a village. It feels a bit like upsetting friends.' She pulls a face.

'I can imagine,' I say, now dreading it a little more. 'So, have you judged similar contests?'

'Occasionally, yes. Last year, we had a Christmas cookie competition right here in the bakery.'

'Here?' I look around doubtfully, as the shop seems so small.

'Out the back,' she explains, noting my puzzled look. 'I will show you, if you like.'

She leads me behind the counter and through a door to a vast space that has me gasping. A large central wooden island is surrounded by colourful stools and flanked by huge shiny ovens.

'I extended. There was no need for the yard outside.'

'Wow, I'm impressed, it looks amazing,' I say, as I take it all in.

'Thank you. By the way, my name is Penny.'

'Pleased to meet you, Penny, I'm Ruby,' I say, introducing myself formally.

I tell her all about my Saturday job here, as a young woman.

'Really? A bit before my time, so I don't remember the previous owner. Shame you're not staying; I could do with an extra pair of hands when it gets busy.' She laughs. 'Although I do have a part-time worker who should be arriving any time now.' She glances at her watch.

After leaving the bakery, pleased to have found a place that sells my favourite pistachio buns, I cross the road to the church.

A smile spreads across my face at the scene of the nativity housed in a wooden shelter, the figures almost life size. Next to it, the Christmas tree is strung with baubles and salt dough decorations made by the children in the village school. The sight of it fills me with a sudden feeling of Christmas cheer.

My mind wanders back to my own childhood, and the nativity play that was always held in the church and its grounds. I felt such pride when I played the part of Mary, having been elevated from my two previous Christmases as a shepherd and an angel respectively and thrust into the full spotlight of the audience. As I think of it, I can almost smell the faint mustiness of the costumes that were pulled from a cupboard in the hall every year by our class teacher.

After the annual school play, shepherds, angel and animal costumes would be hung on a rail covered in a black bin liner, ready for the following year. Not like in a lot of places these days, when nativity costumes appear in the supermarkets, ready for the onslaught of busy parents eager to buy them ready made and brand new.

I am taking in the nativity scene, still recalling the pride I felt when I played Mary, when a voice pulls me out of my daydream.

'We will have to stop meeting like this.' As I turn around, I see Will. He is wearing a padded brown jacket, jeans and brown leather boots. His hair is a little windswept, giving him a slightly wild, but undeniably sexy look.

'We certainly will. What are you doing here?' I ask, briefly wondering if I am the victim of a stalker. This is not his village after all and yet here he is again.

'Just looking at a possible site for one of my housing projects.'

'Oh right. Somewhere nearby?' I ask, thankful that it appears to be a coincidence running into him again so soon.

'Not too far from here,' he says vaguely. I glance around at the distant fields, where there is certainly room for development, but I can't help but feel that it would ruin the landscape, just like we discussed during our conversation at his home when we first met. How much more green land can be built on, I wonder?

'People are in need of houses,' he explains, as if reading my mind.

'I guess so,' I reluctantly agree.

'And it gives the second generation a chance to buy a home in their own village.'

'I get that, you don't need to convince me. Even though it's a pity that some of this God-given land will have to be sacrificed.' It really does seem a shame.

'So, are you heading into the church?' he asks, changing the subject.

'I might do actually. I was just admiring the nativity scene first. I don't think I have seen anything like it elsewhere. Apart from in the *Home Alone* movie.'

'It's quite something, isn't it?' says Will as he admires the giant statues.

'It's wonderful,' I say, surprised at the stirring of emotion I feel as I take it all in, and recall the first time I admired it as a child, with Mum and Dad.

'I have always loved this church.' He glances up at the church tower. 'I like to go in and light a candle for my mum, if ever I am over this way. She passed away a few years ago.'

'That's a nice thing to do.' I smile, thinking that I will do the same thing for my dad.

Inside, there are one or two people in the church praying, so we silently head towards the copper candle stand, both of us selecting a candle and lighting one. There are fresh floral displays of wildflowers around the church and a hint of polish, which has left the pews and wooden altar gleaming.

Although I am not particularly religious, I take a seat for a few seconds and say a silent prayer for Mum to keep her safe on her travels. I hope the people she encounters are good people – then realise I am thinking like the mother, who might worry when their child goes off travelling, rather than the daughter. I also pray for all those poor souls who are suffering in the world right now.

Once outside, Will offers to take me for a coffee, and I accept. What else am I going to be doing, other than checking my phone for updates on the trains? Not to mention feeling slightly nervous at the thought of judging the gingerbread competition in the village hall.

We cross the road to the high street and enter a cosy café with chunky wooden tables. The walls are painted cream with a forest mural along the back wall, and cream pendant lights. A bookcase at one end is lined with books, and one or two people are ensconced on comfy-looking leather chairs, reading. I could imagine myself curled up there with a good book.

'This is a lovely idea, having a reading area,' I tell the proprietor as she delivers our coffees to a table.

'I think so.' She beams. 'I don't mind people sitting reading as long as they buy a drink,' she says, as the tinkle of the door alerts her to new customers. 'Some people think that there should be a café in the library over the road, but then I suppose

I would have competition.' She winks. 'Then again, the days of the library might be numbered...'

Am I imagining things, or did she just give Will a forced smile?

I am about to ask her why she thinks that, when my phone rings.

'Sorry, I need to get this,' I tell Will as I head outside for a second, never one to conduct my business in a café.

'Flooded?'

'Yes,' the administrator of the village hall tells me. 'The heavy rainfall last night following the snow has leaked through the roof of the village hall. The whole place is sodden.' She sighs. 'Those loose tiles should have been fixed long ago,' she says in frustration. 'We have started the cleaning-up process, and there are heaters on full blast, but I am afraid it isn't enough.'

'So what now?' I ask.

'There is no choice but to postpone the gingerbread competition until tomorrow, I am afraid,' she tells me. 'At the earliest.'

'Tomorrow?' Surely this can't be happening.

After my call, I head back inside the café that offers welcome warmth after standing outside. When our drinks are almost finished, I feel reluctant to head outside again into the bitter cold – but I urgently need to speak to someone.

'Can you excuse me for five minutes? I will be back, I promise. Oh, and it looks like I will be staying here for another evening. The gingerbread competition has been postponed until tomorrow,' I tell Will.

There is a small queue of customers at the bakery, so I wait patiently until they have all been served, before I tell Penny all about the flooded village hall.

'I can't imagine it will be even ready by tomorrow... Ideally,

I would have liked it over with today so I could head off, but I guess these things happen.'

'Hmm, I don't suppose a damp, musty-smelling hall would be particularly festive,' she agrees. 'And I think some more snow is forecast this evening.'

'No, really?' I sigh, thinking of those loose roof tiles at the village hall

'I guess with enough help from volunteers, I could host it here,' suggests Penny, which I had been hoping she would.

'But that sounds perfect! I will let Cath at the village hall know; she will get the ball rolling.'

'Happy I can help. We could schedule it for two p.m., give us a chance to set up after the morning rush,' she suggests, as a customer enters the shop.

I call Cath at the hall who is cock-a-hoop at the news, and I return to the café with a new spring in my step.

'Sorry about that,' I apologise to Will.

'No problem,' he says amiably. 'And as you are here for another evening, I was wondering if you would like to join us for dinner.'

'You and Henry?' I ask.

'And our neighbours,' he adds, as he drains the last of his coffee. 'Henry is at their house now. He said it was too cold to come out for a walk.' He grins.

'Oh right, thanks...' I'm a little surprised by his invitation. 'Will you be doing the cooking?' I ask, curious if there is a partner at home.

'Well, Dad certainly won't be.' He grins. 'And don't worry, I won't be serving you any burnt offerings.'

'So, no other half then?' I ask out of interest, thinking of the woman at the Italian restaurant last night.

'What? Oh no, resolutely single. Or more accurately,

divorced,' he reveals. 'The lady at the restaurant last night was Sally, my neighbour. She joined us last night as her husband was out on his Christmas golf outing,' he explains.

'Right,' I say, feeling inexplicably intrigued at the news he is not married. 'Well, I was keeping my eye on train updates, but as nothing appears to be changing, why not? I'll be staying on at the pub.'

'Great news. Not about the train situation obviously. But I am glad you can join us.'

I am beginning to think ahead that I will need to book a taxi, when Will tells me he will arrange a cab to collect me from the pub at seven.

'If that suits you?' he asks. 'I would collect you, but I will up to my arms in food prepping.' He winks.

'Yes, that's fine, I look forward to it,' I say, realising that I actually am.

Outside, the cold air hits my face and as I pass the village hall out trots a face I haven't seen for many nears.

'Marilyn, gosh it is you, isn't it?' I ask the woman standing in front of me. I am suddenly nine years old, sitting on a rug in the church presbytery and listening to the parable of Jonah and the whale.

'It is indeed.' She smiles before wrapping me in a hug. 'How are you, Ruby?' She pushes me at arm's length and appraises me. 'You look wonderful.'

'I'm fine – and you look great too; you have barely changed.'

Apart from her hair being cut into a short, slightly spiky style, and dyed a soft pink, she is just as I remember her. She is wearing some rather fetching gold-rimmed glasses.

'I am so glad I have run into you,' she says warmly. 'Someone mentioned seeing you last night at Roberto's, so I was heading over to the Swan to invite you over for supper this evening. I assumed you would be staying there.'

'As it is the only hotel around, I noticed. It seems the Greyhound is now Roberto's.'

'Which is a fabulous addition to the high street,' says Marilyn. 'I simply can't resist their seafood linguine.'

'I can vouch for the food,' I say, recalling the delicious meal I enjoyed there last night.

'Shame about the Greyhound,' says Marilyn. 'But I think its days were numbered. The young ones in the village rarely used it. I don't think there was much call for a pint of best bitter.'

'Or pork scratchings,' I say, and she laughs.

'I'm beginning to think I ought to have called June at the Swan and left a message instead of venturing out, though, as it's treacherous out here,' says Marilyn, who is at least wearing sensible walking boots, in contrast to my fashionable ankle boots.

'You have a point. And thanks for the invite, Marilyn, I would have loved to have come for dinner, but I have literally just made other arrangements.'

'Oh, that's a shame. Doing anything interesting?' she asks as she slowly falls into step beside me.

I tell her all about my dinner invitation to Will's house before adding, 'I would love to have a catch-up with you, though, as I will be heading home tomorrow. After the gingerbread competition – which has hurriedly been moved to the village bakery.'

'Yes, I have just heard. Thank goodness for Penny coming to the rescue like that.'

I don't tell her that it will also minimise any chance of seeing Nathan if I am in and out of Brindleford. It's already a nuisance that I even have to stay an extra day. Saying that, I am looking forward to dinner this evening. There is something very captivating about Will's company.

'I heard Will Sutton was in town last night…' she comments. 'At Roberto's.'

News travels fast around here, reminding me how things work in a village. So, she knows his surname, which is more than I do. I recall all the stares from the diners too.

'You know him?' I ask her.

'I do. As do most people around here,' she informs me.

'Ah of course, I guess that's because he builds sustainable housing.' I nod. 'I imagine it's quite a godsend for locals who want to live here, having the chance to buy some affordable accommodation.'

'Probably.' She nods.

Perhaps Will is a bit of a local hero and that's why he attracted so many glances as he was leaving the restaurant last night. There's no denying he is seriously attractive too. Come to think of it, I noticed one or two people whispering behind their hands.

'So, do you still run the Sunday school for the children?' I ask Marilyn. I remember always looking forward to the drink and the biscuits at the end, more than the actual scripture.

'Not anymore. Sadly, a lot of people don't like children having Bible stories read to them, even though they teach good morals. Goodness knows we could do with some, the state the world is in.' She shakes her head.

'You're not wrong there.'

'I did marry the vicar, though,' she tells me casually.

'You did! Do you mean Gerard?' I ask. He was known as Father Johnson when I was growing up. 'Assuming he is still the vicar here?'

'He is indeed, and yes, he is now my husband.' She beams at me.

'Well, that is good news. I always liked Gerard.'

'Me too. I think it's the uniform.' She winks mischievously and has me giggling.

I recall Marilyn always having a twinkle in her eye. I'm pleased to see it hasn't diminished over the years. I am also surprised that she has married, after being sworn off men for many years, following a disastrous engagement where her partner disappeared overnight, never to be seen again, according to my mum.

'Anyway, regarding Will's building projects, you are right in saying they have been welcomed in the past, that's true enough,' she explains as we slowly walk along. 'But there are rumours that his latest venture might not prove to be quite so popular.'

We have stopped outside the toy shop, and I glance at the wonderful display in the shop window. Doll's houses, toy trains and old-fashioned wooden pull-along toys grace the window display, the glass edged with bright red tinsel. There are even a few sledges propped up against a wall, and I have a vision of children whizzing down the nearby snow-covered hills.

'What do you mean, with this latest venture?' I ask, intrigued.

'There have been rumours that the local library might be under threat. Apparently, the council are suggesting that the library is not being used enough. And with a limited budget, it might have to go.' She sighs. 'The land would be up for grabs.'

'So the library really could be closed? Surely not.'

'I'm afraid so, and the word is, the council are not opposing the idea. It is no secret that they are keen to have more housing in the village. Will Sutton is very interested in buying the land, so I hear.'

'Land? The village would lose its library and the building itself?' I'm shocked. Surely Will would not be interested in having any part of that?

So I could have been spot on sensing the café owner giving Will a strained smile earlier.

'I'm afraid so. As well as the children's playground next to it. Nothing is set in stone yet, but apparently the wheels are in motion.'

I'm completely shocked by this news. Will never mentioned

the land for the proposed housing being on the site of the library, when I asked him if it was around here. And the little park too, where me and my friends would spend many an evening as teenagers, hanging out and having a laugh, sometimes furtively sharing a bottle of cider.

'But he will have a fight on his hands, that's for sure,' Marilyn says firmly. 'Along with the village hall the library has been the hub of the village for as long as I remember.'

'Gosh, yes I remember it growing up too.' I nod. 'Surely the village needs a library? The nearest one is miles away in Skipton.'

'Exactly. Anyway, I have already been in touch with the council, but they are saying very little... Our local councillor did say that a few libraries in the area are closing down due to lack of funding and under-usage, which I find hard to believe. The government say they worry about the standard of literacy in this country, but if kids cannot access free books from libraries, then things are hardly likely to improve, are they?'

'I couldn't agree more,' I say.

Story time was such a big part of growing up as a young child. Picture books would be read to us, fuelling our imagination, as we sat cross-legged and completely absorbed in the story on Saturday mornings. When I left school, I would ask the librarian to order in some study books for my college course, which she happily did. Marilyn is right, access to books is essential. Surely Brindleford can't lose its library?

'Anyway, are you coming in?' she asks, gesturing to the door of the toy shop. 'I want to grab one of those sledges before they sell out.'

'Who for?'

'Myself, who else?' She chuckles. 'There is no better way to remind yourself that you are not past it than whizzing down a hill. And then the best bit? A big slug of brandy afterwards.'

'I am almost tempted.' I smile as we head inside and the

familiar smell and layout of the shop takes me back to my childhood.

There are teddy bears, and stuffed toys lining shelves alongside board games. Several prams stand in a corner, complete with sleeping dolls. Vintage-style wooden toys take up the rest of the space, although a small section of the shop is home to Barbie dolls and electronic gadgets, bringing it into the twenty-first century.

My instinct is to cancel my evening with Will and take Marilyn up on her invitation to dinner at the vicarage. She is such engaging company, and it has been a long time since I had a proper conversation with the vicar, who was so kind to me and Mum after Dad died.

I even ponder purchasing a sledge and joining her on the hills. But I would like to know a little more about Will's plans to build houses on the site of the village library. And why on Earth the local council is prepared to even consider them? Despite Will being such charming company, surely I owe it to the villagers to try and find out a little more about his proposed building plans whilst I am here?

'Red or blue?' Marilyn asks, eyeing the sledges with a grin on her face.

'Definitely red!' I reply instantly. 'I'd say it matches your energy.'

ELEVEN

I dreamt of the library last night.

I saw my younger self, spending hours poring over books, then carrying them to the librarian, who stamped the ones I had selected to take home.

As I was an only child, the characters in the books became like friends to me, and I would even have conversations with them in my bedroom. My mother would laugh, but Dad would tell me that friends did not have to be real, and didn't Mum feel she knew all the characters from her favourite soaps? He always got me.

The smell of the library came back to me in my dream, along with the faces of some of the locals asking me questions about my college course – a time when I would sit for hours poring over books and studying.

After waking, I had a strong desire to try and help in the fight to save the library. Surely future generations cannot be denied the opportunity to fall in love with books from an early age, or have a place to study for their future?

Bleary-eyed, I head down to breakfast.

'Morning, honey, I hope you slept well!' June beams. 'What can I get you?'

'Just coffee please.'

'So, you are not going for our famous full English breakfast this morning?' she asks cheerfully.

I am almost tempted to decline, in favour of a giant croissant from the bakery across the road, but I feel suddenly ravenous.

'Oh, go on then,' I say after getting a sniff of the breakfast just delivered to a nearby table.

'It's been the talk of the village, you know, you coming to judge the gingerbread competition,' June tells me excitedly. 'I watch you all the time on *Britain's Best Cook*.'

'You do? I hope you enjoy it.'

'Oh, I do. It has given me lots of inspiration for the dining room menu. Although it's my husband who does most of the cooking, which is why you never really see him out here. I am more of the ideas person.' She chuckles. 'Anyway, here I am, blathering on; I had better go and get you that coffee.'

'So, I believe you grew up here.' June places a fresh pot of coffee in front of me.

'I did. I Left for London when I was eighteen.' I pour some coffee from the chrome pot. It smells delicious. 'So how long have you been the proprietor here?'

'Just over five years. We had a pub in Leeds for years, before this came up. Very different I can tell you, but I love it here. I like how everyone knows each other.' Brindleford always has been a special, tight-knit community. 'And hubby is pleased to have found someone to play *Dungeons and Dragons* with, on our board games evenings.'

I love that they still encourage board games and have an actual games evening here. It feels good to know that they have not broken with tradition and installed some huge television to blare out across the pub.

'Are the games evenings popular, then?'

'They are. Admittedly, not too many young people are interested. I blame mobile phones,' she says with a shake of her head. 'But we have some games aimed at younger kids who play with their families, so you never know, we may be nurturing a new generation,' she says hopefully.

She disappears then, to welcome a young couple into the breakfast room, humming as she goes.

Glancing around the dining room, I observe the different types of people, from families who are possibly visiting people in the area or just taking a Christmas break in in the countryside, to young couples, gazing lovingly at each other over their morning coffee.

I never imagined I would be single over Christmas, and I feel a small pang of regret. At least being away from London is distracting me from thinking about it too much.

I thank June, who places the delicious-looking cooked breakfast in front of me, on a blue willow pattern plate, before she dashes off, quietly singing 'Fly Me to the Moon'.

Fully set up for the day with the hearty breakfast, I wrap myself up and decide to take a walk.

Even though the snow has stopped falling, it is a little slippy underfoot after the rainfall last night. I take a left turn at the library and cross the road until I come to a row of brick cottages that date back almost two hundred years.

I take in the row of sandstone houses, their small front gardens covered in the almost melted snow. I stand for a few minutes, just staring at our old house, number twenty-four Daffodil Grove, and I am immediately transported back in time. I can picture the house at Christmas, the tree with the multicoloured lights in the window, and me playing with the kids next door, as if it were yesterday. During the spring, clumps of daffodils would pop up in front gardens and alongside the river that runs through the village.

I find myself wondering if my old childhood friends have moved on, or if they still live nearby? My mind drifts back to New Year's Eve in days gone by, where Dad always insisted on hosting a huge party and inviting the whole neighbourhood, that would include my friends. It would go on until the early hours, and I would discover Dad sleeping in the armchair and wearing a paper party hat when I came downstairs the following morning, my mum bustling about around him tidying up.

I thrust my hands deep into my pockets and move on, lost in my thoughts. I wonder what Dad would make of my swish apartment in London? I like to think he would be proud of me. I know Mum is – although it took a long time for her to tell me so. Well, kind of tell me. One evening when we were having drinks together at my apartment, she glanced around and told me that I had done very well for myself. It was enough.

Back in my hotel room, I change and before I know it, it's time to head off across the road to the bakery. It is a little before one when I arrive, suppressing a feeling of nerves, to find a small crowd clutching phones and maybe hoping for a selfie. I duly pose for a couple of photos and sign some autograph books for older people before heading inside. It still feels strange doing such things, and I am not sure I will ever get used to it. I admit to a good feeling inside, though, at the sight of the happy faces who have turned out to greet me.

As soon as I step into the bakery, a group of people burst into applause under a banner bearing the words *Welcome Back Ruby Holmes* in bright colours. I'm so overwhelmed that 'Oh wow' is all I manage to mutter.

I take in the long trestle table at the rear of the bakery, laden with gingerbread offerings that I will taste very soon and declare a winner. More recently, it was decided that anything made from gingerbread could be entered, and I am impressed with the highly imaginative offerings, from traditional houses to a flower garden, and a whole gingerbread family. I suddenly feel a level of responsibility more than anything I have experienced in the dizzy heights of television, as I prepare to judge the baked goods. The bakers have put their hearts and souls into their creations after all.

Someone local will also assist in the judging, which makes me feel a bit better. Surely no one would have a problem with a pillar of the community choosing a winner?

'Hi, Ruby, lovely to see you again!' Marilyn is dressed in a brightly coloured, floral blouse and jeans. Her glasses of choice today are pink rimmed and match her hair. She is nothing like how you would imagine a vicar's wife to look, but then maybe times really have changed.

'I hope you like the banner; the children made it.' She smiles proudly, pointing to the children's handiwork draped behind the counter.

'I love it! I feel very honoured.'

It is lovely to see Marilyn happy and settled; she certainly deserves to be. Along with the Sunday school, I remember her quietly assisting at the village hall and selling crafts at local markets. She also ran a vintage clothes shop for a short while on the high street, which I noticed is now closed, the bookshop café now in its place.

'The rents were getting a bit much,' she tells me when I ask her about it. 'The town council should be encouraging new business, but I guess it's the same across high streets up and down the country.'

'I think maybe you are right, hence the growth in online businesses. And retail parks.'

'Such soulless places,' she replies with a shake of her head. 'So how is your mum doing?'

'She's okay, currently in Kenya volunteering at an animal sanctuary.'

'I can imagine her doing that – she loved her job as a veterinary nurse back in the day.'

Mum and Marilyn were friends and would go into Skipton together to do some shopping or visit the cinema. She had other friends in the village too but chose to cut herself off from a lot of people after Dad died. When Mum moved away, she and Marilyn kept in touch for a while, but the friendship is nowhere near the way it once was, despite Marilyn's attempt to keep it rekindled, I suspect.

'It really is good to know that you have done so well for yourself. Do you enjoy your work?' Marilyn asks with genuine curiosity.

'Most of the time, yes, I love it, although it can involve long hours and play havoc with your private life,' I find myself telling her.

'So, no boyfriend then?'

'Not currently, no,' I admit. 'And I have no intention of looking for one – I am far too busy with my job.'

'Well, you don't necessarily have to go looking for a partner. Someone usually comes along when you are least expecting it. I never imagined marrying again after my one disastrous relationship as a young woman,' Marilyn reveals. 'But Gerard is just such a lovely man.' She smiles warmly at the mention of his name. 'They say the right one for you is often right under your nose the whole time.'

Our conversation is interrupted then, as a formidable-looking woman in a navy suit taps a microphone and makes a formal introduction. Marilyn tells me she is founder of the newly formed Women's Institute, when I ask. Apparently, the old club had all but folded, but lately there are lots of younger mums keen to learn how to knit clothes and make Victoria sponge, so it appears to be enjoying something of a resurgence.

'And so, without further ado, I would like to welcome Ruby Holmes to join me, in our very own village bakery, that she was once so familiar with,' introduces the lady, her face breaking into a smile that transforms her face. 'And of course you will be ably assisted in your decisions by local farmer and amateur baker Nathan Woods.'

I can hardly believe my eyes, as I watch Nathan push his way through the crowds to the sound of applause, before he takes his place beside me. And amateur baker, really?

'Oh wow, what a welcome,' I address a sea of faces, scanning the crowd for anyone familiar as my heart hammers in my chest. Is Nathan really here to assist with the judging? Did he know I would be judging too? Surely not, otherwise I'm sure he would never have agreed. I did answer late, because I was ill... Perhaps he was their back-up, and then when they finally heard back from me, it was too late for him to pull out.

I spot several people I recognise, who are much older now, but otherwise the crowd is mainly children and, it would also appear, younger couples who must have bought houses and settled here in the village.

'Firstly, may I thank you for welcoming me back here. Back home,' I tell the assembled crowd, some taking pictures with their camera phones. 'I have been reminded what a wonderful village Brindleford is, and clearly still a thriving community. Maybe more so than ever,' I add.

'We are indeed a thriving community,' Nathan confirms. 'Moving with the times. There is something here for everyone,' he says proudly. 'The people of the village are always here to help each other out in a crisis, so let's hear it for Penny for stepping up and saving the competition at the eleventh hour. And, of course, everyone involved in helping.'

'Hear, hear!' shouts someone in the crowd.

Nathan leads the crowd into thunderous applause.

'Well, I, for one, simply cannot wait to taste all these wonderful gingerbread creations,' I continue, keen to get this over with. 'Although they are so pretty it seems almost a shame to eat them. There is nothing like home-made confectionery,' I tell the crowd. 'So may the best gingerbread win!'

'You never told me you were going to be a judge here today,' I whisper to Nathan as I head towards the table to the sound of more applause.

'You never asked.' He shrugs.

He is dressed in jeans, and a smart checked shirt, and the hot guy in the Christmas movie I watched pops into my head.

A little girl tugs at my coat sleeve, distracting me out of my flustered state. 'I've seen you on the telly.' She grins. 'I watched your cookery show with my mum the other night,' she informs me.

'Did you?' I smile at the rosy-cheeked girl who is wearing a red dress.

'Yes. She said you would be here today, but I didn't believe her. Nobody famous ever comes here.' She pouts.

'Well, I am here. And I am pleased you enjoyed the cookery show.'

'I did... Mum said we might make the Christmas chocolate brownies, but without the gold leaf on the top. But then, they are not really Christmas brownies, are they, without gold?' She frowns, and even though she may be right about them not being festive-looking without the glitter, I believe that some things should not be tampered with. I recently saw a viral craze suggesting glitter gravy for Christmas lunch, which is something I will most definitely not be trying.

'Pippa, come away.'

A young woman takes the little girl by the hand and apologises, before hurrying off.

I inhale the unmistakeable smell of ginger, spices and treacle, as we approach the table, and I look forward to taking my first bite of the confectionery.

Some offerings on display are traditional houses, one adorned with a dusting of red edible glitter on the roof, the doors and windows drawn on simply with an icing pen. Another is a flashback to a different decade, with peaks of stiff icing creating a snowy rooftop complete with Santa, snowman, trees and red robins.

A gingerbread family make me smile, as does an impressive garden complete with tall trees and a bench. There is an accurate replica of the village hall, and I realise what a bunch of talented bakers there are here in Brindleford. They would all make worthy contestants on *The Nation's Best Baker*.

I take a bite of a rather delicious slice of moist, fragrant gingerbread, before making my way around the table and sampling everything that is on offer. Nathan joins me in the tasting, and I can feel all eyes on us, as we make our way around the display. His closeness is stirring something in me, something I'm not ready to acknowledge.

'I think this may be one of my more pleasant jobs,' I remark, trying to keep the conversation light. 'Some of this gingerbread is truly delicious,' I say, savouring the tasty gingerbread.

'As good as you can get in London?' asks Nathan with a raised eyebrow.

'Oh please.' I roll my eyes. 'You ought to try the pastries in a place near my apartment. They are melt-in-the-mouth fabulous.'

'Oh I have heard everything about those artisan bakeries,' replies Nathan. 'Almost a tenner for a Danish pastry that probably costs a quid to make. If that.'

'You prefer yours wrapped in a doily then, sold alongside sacks of potatoes?' I retort.

'You've changed,' he says with a shake of his head, and I am not sure if he is joking.

Truthfully, though, some of this home-made gingerbread is some of the best I have ever tasted. Not that I tell Nathan this.

'One of the church volunteers generally bags first prize,' Nathan whispers. 'But I don't think her gingerbread is quite up to scratch this year.' He chews thoughtfully. 'There is a little too much ginger, and not enough treacle,' he decides, and I wonder when he turned into Paul Hollywood.

He leans over to try another piece of gingerbread, and when our hands go for the same plate and briefly touch, a bolt of electricity shoots through me.

Eventually, we place the cards with the winners in front of their offerings. My heart is thumping, and I wonder what on Earth is going on here. I just want this to be over with so I can head back to the place I now call home.

I take the microphone and invite the winner, one Esme Jones, onto the stage to collect her trophy and a hamper of Christmas treats.

'Wow, I can't believe it, thank you so much! I think there was a lot of stiff competition, as all of the gingerbread creations looked marvellous,' she says kindly, and I observe a couple of clearly disappointed faces, who force a smile as the crowd bursts into applause.

Esme – who is around my age and a bubbly redhead – is the creator of the sleek, unfussy house with the red roof, that hands down tasted better than anything else on the table.

'Gosh, this is amazing, I never win anything,' she says excitedly. 'Thanks again.' She raises her trophy aloft and the little girl who had talked to me earlier jumps up and down excitedly beside her, as along with the trophy, there is a hamper prize containing a bottle of mulled wine, some hot chocolate and marshmallows.

Bottles of mulled wine and wooden baking spoons are also handed out to second and third place.

Watching Esme with her daughter makes me fleetingly

wonder if I will ever have a child to attend fetes with and feel the magic of Christmas.

'Right, see you later, then.' Nathan disappears with his phone glued to his ear, after answering a call.

'Your gingerbread really is amazing,' I tell Esme as I try to gather my thoughts. I am not sure what just happened there, or why I feel a twinge of disappointment that Nathan has disappeared without a backward glance.

'Thanks. I must admit, I have been doing a lot of baking lately with my daughter, as well as gifting cakes and biscuits to friends and family. I got some inspiration from the cookery show you hosted. And, of course, from the bakery here.'

Hosting the show briefly inspired me too, but with so many good bakeries on my doorstep in London, I rarely feel the need to roll up my sleeves and get stuck into some home baking.

Being here reminds me of how much I used to enjoy it, though. It was a good way to de-stress after a hectic day, although I often had no one to gift the bakes too, other than my work pals. I barely know my neighbours after all. There would be a host of grateful recipients around here, I'm sure, and requests for cakes for school and village fetes. It is another reminder of the sense of community here.

'The bakery here is fabulous, isn't it?' I agree. 'And it was so nice that Penny stepped up and agreed to host the competition here.'

'It's the least I could do,' Penny pipes in as she passes by and overhears. 'Plus, it pays to advertise.' She winks. 'I have already had one or two people sign up for the new bread-making classes after Christmas.'

'Would you mind if I have a photo with you?' an older lady tentatively asks as she approaches the table. 'I will send it to my sister who lives in Liverpool. She is a big fan of your shows.'

I duly oblige, and it inspires several other people to ask of a selfie together. Maybe I really am a little more famous than I ever realised...

TWELVE

'So, do you live in the village?' I ask Esme.

After posing for selfies and signing autographs, which still feels a little surreal to me, Esme and I are sitting on stools around the huge kitchen island, sipping cups of tea. I am still getting over the shock of Nathan being here, and how being close to him made me feel, so the soothing tea and pleasant company are a welcome distraction. People mill around us, enjoying the stalls set up along the back wall of the kitchen, including the ever-popular tombola, so it's like the fete has come here too.

'I do. We bought a house here a few years ago after deciding to get out of the city, slow the pace a little,' she tells me.

'Which city?' I ask, unable to quite detect her accent.

'Leeds. We were there for five years, and before that Manchester. I was born in Ireland, though, and lived there as a child,' she explains.

'And how is it working out for you living in a village?' I ask, thinking of how I did the exact opposite, and moved to the city all those years ago.

'It's wonderful. I love the sense of community, and Pippa

has made some lovely friends. The village school is adorable, and it's nice that her teacher really knows her, unlike in her last school,' she says, helping herself to a shortbread biscuit. 'The classes were so huge, it must have been hard for the teachers to give the kids the attention they deserved,' she reflects.

For a second I imagine myself with a child in the local primary school, sitting in the same classroom I once did, and feel a rush of warmth.

'Look, Mummy.' Pippa returns clutching a brown teddy with a tartan ribbon around its neck, that she won on the tombola.

'How lovely,' says Esme. 'It seems we are both winners today, then!'

Pippa takes a sip of orange juice before dashing off again to explore the stalls, including a second-hand book and toy stall.

'I can understand that. I guess there are advantages and disadvantages in both places,' I say, thinking of the opportunity for theatre and culture in the capital, not to mention better job prospects.

'No doubt, but I think a village is a nice place to raise a child,' she says, and I suppose I must agree. I had a wonderful childhood here in Brindleford, going on long walks and running free in the hills. We always played together in a group, so our parents never worried too much. When it came to events like Bonfire Night and Halloween, the excitement was contagious. Everyone in the village would be involved in one way or another to ensure a memorable time was had by all.

'So what brought you to Brindleford in the first place?' I ask.

Esme tells me her husband John is a paramedic and burnt out working in a city. While she worked all hours at clothes shop she owned but barely broke even with the cost of renting the space.

'It was a no-brainer to come here. John's grandparents once lived here, and they always spoke so fondly of Brindleford. We now live closer to both sets of parents, who are in sheltered accommodation a couple of miles away.'

'That does make sense.' I nod. 'What do you do for work now?'

'I have an online fashion business, which not only cuts out the high street costs but means I can be around to collect Pippa from school.'

'That sounds perfect,' I say as I sip my tea.

'It works for me. I sell pyjamas and leisurewear mainly, which thankfully are proving to be very popular. Especially at this time of year. I am selling lots of festive pyjamas for all the family,' she says, and I picture happy families in matching pyjamas, standing in front of a log fire and posing for a family photograph.

We chat easily, and as I glance around, I notice a mix of age groups mingling.

Maybe it is a nice place to live, if you don't mind everyone knowing your business. And as much as I can see the charm in watching local amateur dramatics in the village hall, I wonder if I would miss having a pre-theatre meal in a restaurant, before enjoying the latest offering from the West End. Despite my reservations, I can see the appeal for someone raising a family. Esme could quite easily become a friend if I lived here. Despite any feelings of nostalgia, though, I outgrew this village a long time ago.

An hour later, after lots more chatting and promises to return soon, I am just approaching the Swan Inn when June strides out onto the High Street, humming, 'It's the Most Wonderful Time of the Year'.

'Oh, hello, love. I'm just heading to the butcher's for some more of those award-winning pork sausages for tomorrow 's breakfast,' she says, 'which, as I recall, you haven't had a chance to sample yet.'

'Well, I am out for dinner tonight, but as you recommend

them so highly, I will try them tomorrow morning before I leave.'

I'd checked the train situation and there had been no further updates, but I'm still holding on to the hope that the situation might change.

'Marvellous.' She blows heat into her hands. 'That's if everything is back to normal, of course,' she tells me.

'How do you mean?' I frown.

'Staff illness, apparently. Half of them have gone down with the norovirus. And what with the snow already causing problems, it seems the service is still significantly reduced.' She says, 'And more snow is forecast for tomorrow.'

I let her words sink in.

'Ooh I didn't think I'd need my gloves, I'm only going to the butcher's, but it's blooming freezing.' She laughs, seemingly oblivious to my frustration. 'Anyway, love, I must go before they sell out. There are more tea bags and coffee in your room.'

I can still hear her tuneful humming even as she trots away to the butcher's.

Norovirus? Snow on the tracks? Give me strength. This trip has brought nothing but delays and problems so far.

I whip my phone out, and sure enough my train has been cancelled until tomorrow morning at least. Dammit.

I consider getting in touch with Henry, although he is staying with his son until after Christmas, so won't be heading home just yet. Perhaps I could borrow his car, and he could take the train home... Yes! That sound like a plan, and didn't his son say he was worried about his father driving all that way anyway?

I can't be here for Christmas, I think to myself as I walk. It's been lovely catching up with Marilyn and getting to know Esme, but I want to spend Christmas back home in London, with Coleen.

I am almost at the Swan Inn, when I hear the toot of a car

horn and a Range Rover pulls up in the road alongside me. I prepare myself to say 'hi' to Will, but as the window slides down, I have to catch my breath.

'We meet again.'

'Nathan, hi!' I say, suddenly feeling a little left footed. I hoped I might be in and out of the village without encountering him again and dredging up more old memories. And how does he still look so handsome? He has hardly aged a bit.

'Sorry we never got much of a chance to chat, me dashing off like that,' he explains. 'I had to take delivery of some farm equipment.'

'It's fine, don't worry.'

He smiles that easy smile.

'I am glad to know you achieved everything you set out to,' he comments without much emotion. 'In London I mean. It seems you are quite the celebrity these days.'

'I don't feel like one, but thanks. And it really has been good seeing you, Nathan,' I say, despite my brain telling me to leave the past in the past.

Then, he looks at me with those gorgeous brown eyes and something jolts inside me. I'm shocked at the effect he's had on me, and how I feel conflicted: part of me wants to stand here and talk to him all day, another part can't get away quick enough.

'Well, it was good seeing you today, Ruby; enjoy your stay here,' he says, before glancing at his watch. 'I had better be off then. Take care.'

'Thanks.' I surprise myself by wishing we could chat for longer. But what is there to say?

He stays put for a moment, his hands on the steering wheel.

'So, will you be around for much longer?' he calls after me as I walk away. 'We could go for a coffee?'

I am slightly taken aback after his snarky comments while we were judging, yet all the same I can feel my heart soar.

Suddenly, I am a teenager again, and he is asking me out on a date to the cinema in the next town. I recall how my heart skipped a beat when he slipped his hand into mine, as we stood in a queue to watch *King Kong*. We had tossed a coin over whether to watch *King Kong* or *Pride and Prejudice* and he had won.

'Yes, I'm staying here,' I say, gesturing to the pub behind me. I can feel the catch in my voice as I speak, my heart racing. I hope Nathan doesn't notice it too. I am waiting for him to ask me for my number, but surprisingly, he doesn't. And there is no way I am offering it to him.

'Great. Well, I will be in touch. Bye, Ruby.' He smiles.

Why does it feel so nice when he says my name?

'Merry Christmas, Nathan.'

I can feel his eyes on me as I walk inside the pub, before he finally drives off.

Once inside, I order a brandy at the bar and down it in one.

'Cold, are we?' June comes into the pub with a bag of shopping and gives me a knowing look.

'What? Oh yes, freezing.' The warmth of the brandy washes over me, helping me to relax. What on Earth was that I felt? It certainly seemed like more than a friendly hello. I am also a little confused. He never asked for my number, yet tells me he will be in touch. And why do I even care?

I can't help but replay our teenage years in my head, when we would sneak around the back of the farm buildings, kissing passionately, hands exploring each other's bodies, yet somehow managing to refrain from going any further. Eventually, having left school, we did once spend the night together at a hotel out of town – some corporate Premier Inn type place as I recall – where we declared our undying love for each other. Even then, I think a part of me wanted more, and despite our heady teenage love, I knew I didn't want to stay in Brindleford forever.

Occasionally, I wonder why I accepted his engagement ring

and smiled when the locals held a surprise party at the village hall. Despite my love for Nathan, things were already beginning to feel a little claustrophobic. People would constantly ask when the wedding was, and some of the older villagers would smilingly ask us if we were looking forward to the patter of tiny feet.

I remember the conflict I felt, genuinely loving Nathan, yet yearning to spread my wings.

'So, you know Nathan, then? I saw you two chatting,' June asks, reminding me once more that nothing goes unnoticed around here.

'Oh yes, many moons ago,' I say casually.

An almighty crashing sound comes from the kitchen then, which thankfully saves me from any more of her questioning.

'Oops, better go.' June dashes off to the kitchen, so I quietly head upstairs to my room.

If I had already checked out, I would never have encountered Nathan, I think to myself as I flop down onto the window seat and consider my options, which I am beginning to realise are very limited. With no way of getting out of here and only days until Christmas, it would appear I am well and truly stuck here.

THIRTEEN

'So how did it go with the gingerbread competition?' Coleen calls me as I debate going for a walk to a pub in the next village – where no one knows me – and knocking back a few gins.

After checking the weather app, though, and discovering that it is a four-mile walk and with the threat of more snow, I decide to give it a miss. Perhaps I could buy a bottle of gin from the supermarket, although the rumour mill might put out the suggestion that I have a drink problem.

'Great actually. The worthy winner was a lovely young woman from the village.' I think once more of how Esme could easily become a friend.

'And how does it feel being back in the village?'

'Do you know, it feels okay. Everyone here is so lovely. I miss London, though.'

'So, are you on the train back?'

'Erm no, not exactly.'

I tell her all about the train situation, and how I am holed up in a hotel. 'And there is more snow to come. I'd forgotten what the winters in Yorkshire are like.'

'Oh, my goodness. But it's nearly Christmas...' she says, as if I don't already know.

'Is it? No, surely not.'

'No need for sarcasm,' she scolds.

'Sorry, Coleen. I just can't believe I am stuck in the back of beyond.' I sigh. 'I was supposed to be in and out, after the competition. I kind of wish I hadn't agreed to come here in the first place...' Especially after feeling so unsettled by the meeting with Nathan, I think to myself.

'Well, it's hardly the back of beyond, surely,' she reasons. 'At least it has a train station.'

'Yes, which is as much use as a fishnet condom,' I say, and she bursts out laughing.

'It's not funny...' I sigh.

'Oh, Ruby, really, it could be a whole lot worse. Surely the village looks pretty at this time of year, and I'm sure the trains will be up and running soon enough. Maybe you ought to just try and enjoy your time there, see it as a mini break,' she says with her usual positivity. 'Sipping a hot chocolate in a snow-covered, cutesy village is something I would kill for right now.'

'Well, you're right that it is pretty... But I would rather be back home. So I take it you are still up to your eyes, then?'

'I'm totally rushed off my feet. I have a last-minute dress to alter – this time it needs taking in as the bride-to-be has lost too much weight,' she tells me. 'I've barely started my Christmas shopping for the big day. And I've left it too late to do an online shop.'

'Probably not the best idea to shop online after last year anyway...'

I remind her of how last year, the supermarket substituted a box of After Eight mint chocolates with four packets of Polo mints, mince pies with blackcurrant tarts, and a gammon joint with a super-sized packet of processed ham.

'Well, okay, point taken. It's my own fault. Christmas has just crept up on us this year.'

'It has. And I don't envy you, with your current workload. Maybe the guests can bring some of the food this year for Christmas lunch,' I suggest. Coleen usually takes on the mammoth task herself and likes everything to be just perfect.

'Oh they are. Mum is cooking the turkey, and my sister is roasting pigs in blankets and parsnips. I am also told my nieces have been baking shortbread.'

'So stop complaining,' I joke. 'Seriously. It's about time you let others lend a hand. You have enough on your plate.'

'You're right. I guess I do put pressure on myself. I just like to have things perfect,' she admits.

'Control freak.' I cough the words and Coleen laughs. 'Anyway, maybe you are right, I ought to enjoy my time here as I am not due back in the studio until the new year.'

'Exactly. Although it's a shame you aren't here to give me a hand with these dresses,' she jokes.

'Do you want to ruin your reputation?' I couldn't sew if my life depended on it.

'Point taken. Anyway, try and enjoy your time there. As I said, see it as a mini break.'

'Maybe I ought to do just that. I could get used to someone serving me a delicious breakfast each morning.'

'Now you are just showing off.' She laughs.

I had vaguely imagined spending a few days on a beach somewhere in the sun during my Christmas break, rather than in a freezing cold Yorkshire village. But sometimes things don't turn out the way you expect them to.

'Anyway, I'm not sure why you are so desperate to leave Brindleford; surely you know a few people there?'

'It's true, I do.'

I tell her all about Marilyn. 'And no doubt there will be

others I may come across, but it's been so long since I lived here, it doesn't feel remotely like home.'

'Well, you will be back in London before you know it, with all its traffic, noise and pollution, so I would enjoy the fresh air up there whilst you can,' she suggests.

'There is that I suppose.'

I don't tell Coleen that I am keen to disappear from the village after running into Nathan – I don't want to relive the moment I saw him. I will tell her all about it when I get home.

The truth is, I never expected my heart to race when I saw him for the first time in almost two decades. In fact, I can barely get the thought of him out of my head after seeing him today.

Who did Nathan marry? Was it someone from the village? Maybe even someone I knew in my younger years? Mum had told me that he dated someone local, the year following our split. I remember my heart sinking a little at the thought of him with someone else, though I'd quickly pulled myself together, reminding myself that it was my choice to move to London.

No, I can't dig up my past here in the village; it wouldn't be fair on me or Nathan. My life is in London and the sooner I return, the better.

If anything is going to distract me from my thoughts of Nathan, though, it is dinner at Will's place later.

I still can't believe Will would be happy to buy the land that the library sits on – could it simply be rumours? I'm really quite devastated at the thought of the library disappearing and houses standing in its place, however great the need for accommodation around here. I may not be here for very long, but I think I ought to assist in any way I can to help preserve the village library.

I make myself a cup of tea, and flick on the small television in my room, mindlessly taking in the quiz show on the screen. It is nice to know that despite the no-TV rule in the pub, the bedrooms have them installed. At least I can lose myself in a film later when I return home.

Finishing my tea, I nip out to the local supermarket for a bottle of wine to take with me to Will's place. As the young shop assistant scans the wine, I wonder what the younger residents think about Will's plans. Maybe they wouldn't mind quite as much, with so much information available online these days, or perhaps they still like to get their hands on a good book. I realise there is only one way to find out. After hopefully finding out a little more this evening, it feels like time to suggest Marilyn calls a meeting at the village hall.

I quickly nip to the village bakery next and purchase a dreamy-looking lemon and raspberry cheesecake to take for dessert that I hope the other guests will enjoy. After purchasing it, I wonder if I should have just stuck to the wine. Maybe Will has been slaving all afternoon preparing a lavish dessert.

All the while, the cogs have been continuing to whirr in my mind regarding the planned site for the new-build houses. As I walk back to the hotel to get ready, I consider calling someone I know who is currently working for a regional TV station in this area, in case the need arises. This story might just need a little bit more publicity. And it might just be the break Amanda Lewis needs.

FOURTEEN

'Ruby, welcome!' Will kisses me on both cheeks as I arrive at his beautiful home. He ushers me inside, and I take in the scent of his expensive cologne. He is dressed in a pink shirt, sleeves rolled up, and navy jeans.

I hand him the bottle of red wine – the best from the limited choice at the high street food store, along with the cheesecake, and he thanks me warmly.

'Great choice,' he says. 'I forgot to defrost a dessert, so was thinking about cheese and crackers,' he tells me, which makes me feel better.

Inside, the guests are assembled on sofas surrounding the roaring log fire. The neighbour who was at the restaurant is accompanied by her husband this evening, and introductions are made.

'So how are you enjoying being back in Brindleford?' asks Henry as we move into the kitchen and are seated at the large dining table.

I ponder his question a minute before I answer. 'To my surprise I have rather enjoyed being back here – at least some aspects of it.'

'Any in particular?' Will asks with a cheeky wink.

Maybe I ought to ramp up the flirting a little. It might distract me from Nathan, and I do find Will attractive, there's no doubting it.

'Visiting the church and the village hall brought back lots of memories...' I sip the deep, rich wine Will had served. 'Oh, and the toy shop was a particular highlight. It's nice to see that some things never change. I am hoping to pop into the library before I leave as that holds lots of childhood memories for me too.'

I glance at Will, who swirls his drink around in his glass and avoids eye contact, his playful smile seemingly vanished.

'So have you seen any old familiar faces?' Henry asks.

'One or two. I was happy to run into Marilyn from the church.'

I tell Henry about seventy-year-old Marilyn buying a sledge and heading for the hills, and they all laugh.

'She sounds inspirational. Shall I get you one, Dad?' Will teases.

'No bloomin' chance.' Henry shakes his head. 'I have managed to get to eighty years of age without breaking any bones; I don't want to risk it now.' He chuckles.

The dinner feels relaxed, with garlic bread and salad on the table. Will tells us to help ourselves as he brings a piping lasagne out of the oven. It really is quite delicious, and when I tell Will, he is very pleased with himself.

'I can relax now.' He grins. 'It may be a simple thing, but a perfect lasagne is hard to nail.'

'I never said it was perfect,' I tease, before taking a sip of my wine.

When dinner is over, Will brings out the cheesecake I bought and talk turns to our respective careers. I learn that Will's guests are retired teachers and enjoying exploring Britain in their camper van. After asking me about my TV career, I decide it's time to approach the subject of Will's latest venture.

'It would appear everyone in the village seems to know you.' I turn to Will. 'Or at least your building work.'

'Been talking about me, have you?' he says, with that cheeky grin.

'Actually, it was Marilyn who mentioned it...' I reply.

'Oh most people in the area know who I am,' he says. 'A few of the other villages around here have at least a dozen of our sustainable houses. As I said, it's a really good opportunity for the next generation,' he states proudly.

'Although it seems a lot of them move away for work,' I remind him. 'There isn't much opportunity for employment in the small villages. So I wondered whether some of the houses are bought up as holiday homes...'

'Not usually.' Will's jaw tightens slightly. 'Besides, some locals are happy to commute to nearby towns for work; but yes, some do move out of the area. At least with affordable housing it gives them a choice.' He shrugs.

A fair point, I guess. Some people do like to remain in the place they were raised in. After all, I would probably have done the same, had it not been for my fierce ambition to pursue a career in the media.

'And Penny is a local girl. Thank goodness she set up that bakery,' he adds, polishing off the last of his cheesecake and making appreciative noises.

'Right, anyone for coffee?' Will stands and I offer to help.

'Not for me, lad, but I'll have a whisky nightcap I think. Might help me to nod off; my back's been playing up a bit today.' Henry winces theatrically as he rubs at it.

'It's a good job I'm driving him back when he leaves,' Will tells me in the kitchen as he busies himself with the coffee machine. 'I had not realised how old he was getting. I do worry about him sometimes.'

'I know what you mean. We think our parents will stay the same forever.' I think of my own mum, who at the moment is fiercely independent. That won't always be the case, though, and I try not to think about it. 'So, you are driving Henry back to London?'

'I am. I'll get the train back here. I have been trying to persuade Dad to move in with me for years, but he is having none of it,' he reveals, as the coffee machine hisses.

I ask him which coffee cups to use, before setting them down on the counter. I am about to suggest I drive Henry home, recalling the journey here not being too bad, when Will reminds me that he will be staying on here for another week.

'But at least he will be here for Christmas and New Year. We have a few things planned – including a New Year's Eve party.'

'That sounds nice.' I smile, thinking it sweet how Will likes to look after his father. Could he really be the type of man to be happy to buy the land that is the site of a library and children's play area? I am about to broach the subject again, when Will picks up the tray of coffees and carries it through to the lounge.

Talk turns to everyone's plans for Christmas Day, and before I know it, it's time to leave. It seems I have missed the chance to do any more digging about the library.

'Thank you for a lovely evening,' I tell Will as he helps me on with my coat. A glance at my watch tells me that the grumpy taxi driver who drove me here will be outside in exactly one minute, and I get the feeling he will be punctual.

At the front door, we stand facing each other for a second, and I can feel Will's masculine presence. He kisses me on both cheeks and thanks me for coming. For a second, I wonder whether he is about to move in for a kiss on the lips, when a beam of light slides along the gravel driveway as my taxi arrives.

'Thanks again,' I say before walking to the awaiting car. I feel a strange sense of relief and disappointment at the arrival of the driver.

Will follows me and opens the door for me. 'I hope I can see you again before you leave,' he says as he leans in close.

'I'd like that.'

I hear my driver cough, so we say our final goodbyes and set off back for Brindleford, my mind in a turmoil. Wasn't I supposed to ask Will directly about his plans? Yet there I was having a perfectly lovely evening, and not pressing Will about his plans, even when we were alone in the kitchen.

I tell myself that it wasn't really the place to be having that type of discussion, and that I will ask him directly about it next time we meet. In the meantime, I have the small matter of telling Marilyn that I have managed to find out absolutely nothing.

* * *

'So how did it go at Will's dinner party?' Marilyn asks the next morning.

She has called in for coffee at the hotel, whilst her husband is hosting a wedding rehearsal with a couple from the village. I can't think of anything more romantic than a Christmas wedding – it's a shame I won't be here to see it.

Today, Marilyn is wearing large, red-rimmed glasses and a rather fetching purple faux-fur coat. Her short hair has been trimmed and with her red lipstick, she reminds me a little of Prue Leith.

'I'm so sorry, Marilyn, I never really found out much,' I tell her truthfully. I hadn't realised just how much I might enjoy getting involved with the villagers and their problems. 'I feel like I have let you down, but it never really seemed like the place to discuss his business affairs. He had other guests, and it was all rather jovial and Christmassy.'

'Oh well, never mind. I suppose the deal is already done.' She sighs, draining her coffee. 'These things usually are, even before they come to the public's attention. That doesn't mean we will not fight for our library, though,' she says with conviction.

'I promise I will speak to him again. Although I'm not sure what good it will do, as I will be on my way home before I know it.'

'What will be will be, although as I said, not without a fight, don't you worry. Anyway, I take it you will be joining us for the nativity later?' she asks.

'The nativity is this evening?'

'It is. It is one of the things I look forward to the most at Christmas.'

'Oh, me too. Yes, I would love to come along, it was always such a joy.'

'No donkeys these days, though' – she winks – 'apart from children wearing outfits.'

We reminisce about the time a donkey defecated on the floor and both roar with laughter.

'Well, at least the children won't do that. Or I hope not.' She nudges me, and I crease up with laughter once more.

'Anyway, don't worry about not finding out much. In all honesty, there is not much you could have done anyway.' She sighs.

'But I at least have to try,' I tell her as we finish our coffee. 'In fact, I know someone at a regional TV station in Leeds. I heard from Sienna that Amanda Lewis is currently covering some local news stories there. Maybe they could come and film the story, if you could get together some protestors.' My mind is working overtime. 'That's how we'll find out for sure. And you know, the council have a duty to tell the public of future house builds in the area.'

I feel a little torn as Will is quickly becoming a friend, but once village libraries start being demolished for new houses, who knows where it will end?

'That's a wonderful idea,' she says, placing her coffee cup down. 'Do you really think you could help?'

'I will if I can,' I promise.

'And I will get a petition started on social media if you like. I don't know why I hadn't thought of it before now, but then the council have been very cagey about actually making an announcement...' she tells me.

'Surely, they must reveal proposed building plans to the public, though?'

'Oh they do. But we don't have a local free paper anymore, which is probably a calculated move to keep us in the dark about everything.' She taps the side of her nose. 'They probably taped the planning proposals to a lamp post in the dead of night or something, to cover themselves. Or maybe it was overlooked, who knows? What I do know is, we cannot lose our library. Especially as they think it is under-used, which is complete nonsense.' She shakes her head. 'The library isn't just for borrowing books; it hosts so many events, including craft clubs, after-school Lego club, and many other activities in the school holidays...' she explains.

I think of the café with the book corner that is charming, but hardly big enough for activities during the school holidays. The more I hear of how the library plays a part in the community, the more outraged I become.

'I will get Gerard to talk to the congregation on Sunday, although the flock is getting rather small, I hate to say.' Marilyn sighs. 'We have our regulars, and one or two curious young families, who have bought houses in the village, but they never seem to return. I've told Gerard that maybe we need to install a coffee machine. His sermons can't be that bad, surely?' She laughs.

'No, of course they aren't,' I reassure her, recalling Gerard's rather animated and lively sermons, often involving role play with unsuspecting members of the congregation. He once chose me – and I've never understood why – to play Jezebel, a biblical harlot, when I was seventeen years old. Maybe he had got wind of my evening away with Nathan at the Premier Inn.

'A coffee machine might not be a bad idea,' I say, only half joking. 'Anyway, I am sure the parishioners will rally the rest of the villagers. And I promise to hear it straight from the horse's mouth exactly what is going on.'

'Wonderful. Perhaps you've been sent to us for a reason.' Marilyn looks heavenward as she speaks.

'Well, I don't know about that, and I can't make any promises.' I smile. 'But of course, I will do my best. To help.'

'I appreciate it. Right, well, I must be off.' Marilyn stands up. 'I have a bit of admin to do for the church. Being a vicar's wife is not all drinking tea and baking cakes.' She winks. 'Bye for now.'

FIFTEEN

I finish my coffee and check my phone for train updates. Still nothing.

At least I am enjoying being here more now and feeling a little less stranded than I did initially – Will might be on a different side, but it's been nice to get to know him, along with some of the younger residents in the village, such as Esme and Penny from the bakery.

I decide to head out off for a walk to pass some time, when from across the road, Esme waves at me.

'Esme, hi, how are you?' I ask, crossing the road to speak to her. She looks stylish in a black and white checked woollen coat, and a burnt orange satchel bag that matches her hair. 'I was just thinking about you.'

'Good thoughts I hope.'

'Of course,' I say as I fall into step with her. 'I was just thinking how getting to know you and some of the other villagers has made my stay here more pleasant.'

'Thanks, that's good to hear.' She grins. 'I am surprised you are still here actually, although I guess the trains have been a bit hit and miss with the weather – and now the train strikes. Fancy doing that over Christmas?' Esme shakes her head. 'Although I guess it makes more impact.'

'Is the train strike definitely going ahead?' I ask.

'Yes. Today. Let's hope there are no further strikes planned in the future.'

'Gosh, I hope not... I hope to be finally on my way back to London tomorrow.'

We chat for a while longer, before she glances at her watch.

'Anyway, I must dash,' she says. 'I have to put the finishing touches on a wedding cake for a wedding on Saturday.'

'That sounds nice. I didn't realise you were a professional baker,' I say, briefly wondering if she ought to have been awarded first prize for her gingerbread house.

'Oh gosh, no nothing like that. It's more of a hobby,' she assures me. 'The bride in question is a friend of mine, who asked me to make her cake. Wedding cakes cost a fortune these days, so it is my gift to the couple.'

'How lovely. She is lucky to have a prize-winning baker as a friend.'

'Thanks. And sorry, but I really must go. I want to get the cake sorted before hubby returns with Pippa. They have a nativity dress rehearsal this afternoon.'

'Of course. See you later.'

'Are you coming to the nativity?' she asks, before heading off.

'Yes, I'll be there,' I tell her, realising I am really looking forward to it. I also surprise myself by feeling unperturbed at the thought of staying here for another evening.

'Great, see you there. Pippa has the part of an angel.' She strides off, waving her hand above her head as she goes.

Pippa certainly has the face of an angel. It makes me think of when I first appeared as an angel, and I wonder how long it will take Pippa to reach the dizzying heights of playing Mary.

My past seems to be assaulting me from all sides the longer

I stay here in the village. I remember walking onto the stage in the church and smiling at Mum and Dad when I played the part of Mary. I never had any lines, but the pride I felt was something I will never forget.

Then, my mind drifts to Nathan, and if he might pop into the church service this evening. Not that it matters. I'll soon be heading back to the place I call home these days. It's probably best not to become accustomed to these village traditions, however charming they might be.

SIXTEEN

I am preparing to head for the church a little after six, when Will calls and asks if he can see me tomorrow morning for coffee at the Swan Inn. I tell him that would be lovely, reminding him it may depend on the train situation.

Tucking my phone into my handbag, I wrap my scarf around me for the short walk to the church.

The temperature has dropped so much that after the recent rainfall, the ground is now hard and frozen. I walk carefully in my flat boots, aware that they're not the most practical footwear and feel relieved when my feet crunch into the gravel of the path leading to the church entrance.

Before I go inside, I stop to take in the impressive Christmas tree once more. I imagine the children sitting at their desks in school and painting the clay and wooden painted baubles, the names of lost relatives etched into them, which I find particularly poignant and beautiful. The bright multicoloured lights still make me smile and it is comforting to know that nothing has changed.

There is an excited chatter as groups of people make their way along the gravel path to the church, one or two mums arriving late with their children, clutching their hands and hurrying them along.

'Ruby, glad you could make it,' says Gerard, shaking me warmly by the hand. He is standing at the church entrance welcoming everyone to the nativity. 'We will talk later.' He smiles, before greeting a middle-aged couple behind me.

Inside, the church is already half full, and I make my way to a pew towards the back, thinking it only fair that the locals who are here to watch their children have the prime seats.

The church has been beautifully decorated with sprigs of holly and ivy along with chunky church candles on window ledges, their flames gently illuminating the vibrant colours of the glass. It occurs to me then that I have never been inside my local church in London, even at Christmas time. I am not even sure where it is.

I am staring at the altar straight ahead, as groups of children begin to file down the aisle from the back of the church. There are audible gasps of admiration from the watching congregation, mainly parents who wave at their little ones as they pass by.

The church is already almost filled to capacity, when an elderly lady with her grey hair in a bun, and accompanied by a young woman, slides into the bench next to me and smiles. As I return her smile, I think I vaguely recognise her from somewhere but can't quite place her.

I am about to speak to her, when a silence falls over the hall, as the headteacher of the nearby primary school welcomes us all and announces the start of the nativity.

The children burst into 'Silent Night', led by a teacher with a pleasant but very high-pitched voice that takes me right back to my primary school days here in the village. I am at once transported to the wooden floor in the assembly hall of my primary school, where we would sit cross-legged, as our teacher played piano and sang at the top of her soprano voice.

The children at the front of the stage look adorable and a

delightful, gap-toothed child of around seven years old stands and narrates, setting the scene in Bethlehem.

Esme, who is in the pew in front, turns to me and points out Pippa standing proudly in a gold angel outfit complete with sparkly tinsel halo.

For a second, I wish Mum was here – she always loved the nativity. When Dad died, she stopped coming, saying she could not bear the looks of sympathy on people's faces when they spoke to her.

As I grew older, I found it quite sad that she chose to live somewhere away from here and take comfort in strangers, rather than old friends. There is no doubt they would have supported her here, but I guess she just needed some time alone.

Everything seems to be going well with the nativity, when a young girl who looks to be around reception class age announces in a loud voice that she needs a wee. When she is quickly ushered off the stage, several other children raise their hand and ask the same thing.

The teacher on stage, clearly forgetting she has a microphone attached to her sweater, mutters something to another teacher about this being ridiculous, and why the bloody hell did the children not need the toilet earlier, when she asked them?

'They never do,' says someone from the audience, most of whom are now giggling, whilst the teacher turns puce with embarrassment.

The headteacher takes control of the situation by telling the children there will be no more toilet visits until the next scene has finished. This results in one child bursting into tears and sobbing theatrically, before being escorted quietly from the stage.

'It was on a starry night...' Pippa sings the first line of a song before the other children join in, as Esme looks on proudly.

A row of smaller children is standing on a bench behind the

older kids, and one little boy appears to be digging another little boy in the ribs. They gently jostle each other, with that mischievous look on their faces that young boys have, when the slightly taller one shoves the smaller boy, who falls off the bench and into the row of children in front. A domino effect ensues with the singing children toppling over one other, whilst admirably still singing.

Most of the children are laughing, one or two are crying, and one little boy in a shepherd's costume is waving at his mum, who I notice taking a sneaky a video of the whole thing on her phone, despite the no photos rule.

'Oh, my goodness,' says the grey-haired lady next to me, clapping her hands in delight. 'This is so much more exciting than last year's performance.'

It dawns on me then where I know the lady from: she had been the landlady of the Greyhound pub.

The teachers hurriedly reassemble the children on stage to the strains of 'The Holly and the Ivy' being played on the piano with gusto.

By now I'm sure the lady next to me is Phylis, who must be at least in her late eighties by now. I wonder what became of her husband, although in all honesty, even twenty years ago, he never exactly looked a picture of health, with his ruddy cheeks and rotund stomach.

Half an hour later, the performance has finished, thankfully without any more hiccups, and the assembled congregation give the children a standing ovation. Before I have a chance to speak to Phylis, the lady sittingnext to Phylis leads her away. I feel sad about missing the opportunity to say hello.

The vicar takes to the stage then, thanking everyone involved. 'Well, that was eventful. But the show went on, didn't it? Thanks to all the wonderful staff of Brindleford primary school, for keeping things moving.' He gives them a round of applause, and the audience join in. 'And of course for all their hard work in this year's nativity. But of course we would not have a show without our wonderful talented children. Well done to every single one of you,' he says, turning to the children on stage, as more applause and a standing ovation follows.

He invites parents to take a photo of their children, reminding them about safeguarding laws and not sharing things on social media. He then tells the congregation that refreshments will shortly be served at the rear of the church hall, should they wish to stay and partake.

'That was entertaining!' Esme chuckles as we enjoy a cup of tea and a mince pie. Lots of families have drifted off, but there are still quite a few milling around chatting and enjoying the melt-in-the-mouth mince pies and shortbread on offer, donated by Penny from the bakery.

'Well done you!' I tell a flushed-looking Pippa, who is glugging down a glass of blackcurrant juice.

'Thank you,' she says politely, before she turns her attention to her friend who is dressed as one of the three kings.

Marilyn joins us for a chat then, along with a few other mums and their children.

'I bet you wouldn't see that in the West End,' she says, as she produces a bottle of mulled wine. She grabs three paper cups, before furtively filling them. 'Not enough to go around,' she explains with a wink. 'It's better warm really, with a nice cinnamon stick, but it will have to do.' She hands us the drinks that we gratefully sip.

'It was a lot of fun.' I smile. 'I had forgotten how the nativity always gets me in the Christmas mood, and the children were brilliant.'

'They were, weren't they?' Esme agrees. 'They manage to pull it off every year, with or without the disasters.' She laughs. 'So, will you be staying here for Christmas?' she asks as we sip our wine.

'No, I don't think so,' I say, although a little less emphatically this time. 'I will be heading off tomorrow.'

'It's not *that* bad here, is it?' She raises an eyebrow and smiles.

'No, not at all. It's just my life is in London. I barely know anyone here anymore, apart from the vicar and Marilyn – although I am very pleased to have made a new friend,' I say, tapping my paper cup against hers.

'Same here. And there are quite a few young people living here nowadays, as I mentioned. Including Penny, who you have already met. We have a walking group, a yoga class at the village hall and regular dinner dates at Roberto's.'

'And of course, we could always do with a more people in our congregation,' adds Marilyn.

'It all sounds very tempting. And I actually went to Roberto's the other night; it was lovely.'

'It is. And a new Thai restaurant will be opening soon on the high street. It's all going on here,' says Esme.

'Really?' My mouth waters at the thought of a pad thai.

'Well, you can join our gang if you do decide to stay on for a bit longer,' she offers kindly, just as Penny arrives and places some more mince pies down, still warm from the oven.

'Thanks, that's nice of you. And the activities do sound lovely,' I say, imagining a forest walk with a bunch of friendly women, or eating food and drinking wine at Roberto's. It reminds me that I don't have a lot of girlfriends back home.

'My friend is getting married here tomorrow; it's a shame you can't be here to see the wedding,' Esme adds.

'I am really looking forward to it,' says Marilyn. 'The church is going to look wonderful, with winter flowers and foliage, and we are putting candles all around the altar. It would be lovely if you could stay…'

'That sounds magical.' I can already picture the scene in the church.

'Hopefully it will be. It really would be marvellous if you could stay – especially as the reception is going to be held at the Swan Inn where you're staying,' Marilyn tells me. 'And wait until you see Esme's cake, it really is stunning!'

'Thanks!' Esme smiles modestly.

'It does indeed sound lovely, but as I don't know the bride-to-be, I'm not sure I would be invited to the wedding...'

'Oh, but everyone is welcome to the church service,' Marilyn explains. 'You know what it's like around here. Although perhaps you have forgotten.'

Maybe I have, I think to myself, as a wedding really does involve the whole village. I remember that from when I was a young girl.

Glancing around the church, it seems that most people have headed off home, something that Marilyn comments on.

'It's a shame people don't seem to hang around churches once the service is over,' she muses, as she looks around. 'Although serving snacks and a drink does at least mean some of them are here long enough for Gerard to push a leaflet about our church services into their hands.' She laughs. 'And maybe we really should consider getting one of those fancy coffee machines.'

'On reflection, the local coffee shop might not thank you for that,' I point out.

'True enough. We will stick to Yorkshire tea and instant coffee.'

As I place my paper cup into a bin, I notice the grey-haired lady once more, pushing a walking frame, and I excuse myself for a moment.

'Pardon me but are you Phylis who once ran the Greyhound pub?' I ask her.

She scrutinises my face for a moment before she speaks. 'My goodness, it's young Ruby, isn't it?'

'It is, maybe not so young anymore, though.' I smile.

'Compared to me you are a spring chicken.' She laughs. 'And you have hardly changed a bit. Yes, I remember you and Nathan.' She smiles.

'You do?'

'Oh yes. I recall you trying to get served once when you were under eighteen.' She frowns in concentration as she recalls the moment. 'I know that because the previous day, your mother spoke of your upcoming eighteenth birthday. It's more than our licence would have been worth to serve you before then.' She smiles at me with kind, watery grey eyes. 'It's funny the things I can recall from yesteryear but ask me what I had for dinner last night, and I wouldn't have a clue.' She laughs.

'I remember trying to get served in a pub when I was underage myself,' says her companion, who introduces herself as Phylis's carer. 'I even had a fake ID. So brazen when I think about it...'

'I guess we were all so desperate to be grown up,' I reply, wondering why on Earth I was so keen to do that – although maybe that is only with hindsight, as the years are flying by far too quickly.

I ask Phylis about her husband as her carer chats to someone else nearby, and she frowns once more before telling me he died some time ago and that she lives in a care home nearby. 'I'm not so good on my feet these days,' she explains, tapping her walking aid.

'I always thought you and young Nathan would marry,' she tells me thoughtfully as she nibbles a shortbread.

'I think most people did,' I reflect, remembering how I proudly displayed my engagement ring to all and sundry. Maybe I truly believed it myself in the beginning, before my desire to move to London and pursue a career truly took over. 'I assume he carried on running Hope Farm, then?' I comment, recalling he was heading out to a delivery the day I ran into him.

'Oh yes.' She smiles. 'Married with two lovely little boys.'

Just then, her carer rejoins us and tells Phylis that they ought to be heading back to the care home.

'Well, it was lovely to see you,' Phylis says, gently touching me on the arm before she departs.

'You too. Take care, and merry Christmas.'

'Merry Christmas, Ruby.'

The news that Nathan is married with two sons inexplicably makes me feel regretful – but what did I expect? After all, it is highly likely that he would be married by now.

Here I am, at almost forty, without a partner and I can't help wondering how different our lives are and if children will ever happen for me? Little boys, Phylis said, so perhaps Nathan only got married in his thirties. Maybe his sons were part of the nativity earlier. I wonder why he was keen to go for coffee if he has a wife and children... but then I suppose there is no harm in simply having a catch-up before I head back to London.

I remind myself of how I felt when I laid eyes on him yesterday, and in this very moment decide that there will be no catch-up over coffee. As soon as this train strike is over, I will be on the next available train out of here.

SEVENTEEN

'Well, it has been lovely staying here, June, thank you for everything.'

I am at the reception desk settling the bill for my stay here at the Swan.

'You're welcome. It's been lovely having you here,' says June warmly. 'You should come back in the spring. The daffodils will be out then, and it's a gorgeous walk into the next village from here – but of course you already know that.'

'You never know,' I say, yet doubting I will return.

I know that walk like the back of my hand, I think to myself, as I imagine turning right at the church, and onto a public footpath, flanked by open fields. The route passes the remains of an old mill before heading into slightly hilly terrain. After walking for around an hour, and passing a farmhouse en route, the distant view of the cove at Malham can be seen. The farm in question is Hope Farm, the home Nathan grew up in.

'And I agree, that walk really is beautiful in spring,' I say.

Thankfully, the trains are up and running today and I have booked my ticket for the two o'clock train, which will give me time to say my goodbyes to everyone. I wasn't expecting to connect with people enough to have to do a round of farewells. It's a bittersweet moment – maybe I should suggest I'll come back next year to judge. I could even bring Coleen.

As I pack my things into my small suitcase, glad that I brought a couple of extra outfits, I feel a little guilty that I was unable to find out any more about Will's plans to build in the village, or indeed offer any more support to the campaign. But Marilyn will be the voice of the people when she finds out for sure, which she tells me she will put all her energy into, once Christmas is over.

I am about to head out, when as if breaking into my thoughts, Will calls.

'Will, hi, how are you?' I ask.

'Good, good. I was just wondering if you were still up for meeting this morning?' he asks. 'I heard the trains are up and running.'

'I am booked on the two o'clock. This afternoon, so sure, why not?'

'Great. And it's good news about the trains. For you at least. If you had been around tomorrow I would have suggested going out for a drink.'

'Oh that's a shame,' I find myself saying.

'So you would have said yes?' he asks. Speaking to him reminds me that he has rather a sexy voice.

'Yes,' I tell him honestly. It would have given me the chance to find out more about his building plans. Plus, being with him certainly takes my mind off Nathan.

'Then perhaps you have time for a bit of a country walk before you leave, instead of coffee at the hotel...?' he suggests. 'I know a little café, newly opened, that does the best hot chocolate.'

'Hmm. Yes, I guess I could. I need to say goodbye to Marilyn and Gerard at the church, though, so maybe in around an hour?'

'Perfect. Although actually, when I say café, it's more of a wooden hut really, but it does have outdoor furniture.'

'In this weather?'

'Fair point. We can always grab a takeaway, keep us warm as we walk.'

'Sounds good. See you later, then.'

Before I head off to see Marilyn, I suddenly think of Henry and decide to give him a call. I would love to meet up with him when he returns to London.

'Henry, hi, it's Ruby,' I tell him when he picks up.

'Ruby, oh hello, love, how are you?' he asks warmly.

'I'm good, Henry, yourself?'

'Oh aye, I'm fine, love, just back from a nice walk actually, got to keep moving at my age, although my jogging days are over.' He laughs.

'I was just calling to let you know that I'm leaving Brindle-ford today. I have your number, so maybe we could meet for a coffee in London sometime?' I suggest.

'I would like nothing more.'

'Great, I will look forward to that, then.'

'Me too. You Have a good journey,' he says before adding, 'Oh, and didn't that lad of mine say he was meeting you this morning?'

'He is, yes; I am just off to say bye to a couple of people first.'

'Well, bye, then, Ruby, but there is just one more thing,' he adds before he ends the call.

'What's that?'

'I'll meet you for a cup of tea, not coffee.' I can imagine him grinning on the other side of the line.

'You're on. I might even buy you a teacake to go with it.'

'Now you're talking.'

When I hang up, I remind myself that new connections can come in all shapes and sizes. Maybe it's time I opened myself up more to the possibility of having more friends in my life.

'For the journey,' says Penny, handing me some chocolate croissants when I pop in to say bye. 'And I was serious about giving you a job, should you decide to stay.'

'Good to know, and thanks,' I say, raising my bag of goodies. 'See you around, take care, Penny.'

'You promise you will come back for the Easter service.' Marilyn is clutching my hand as I prepare to leave. 'And it would be wonderful if you could persuade your mum to come too...'

'I will try my best, Marilyn. You know, I think if she came here, she might remember the good times. And what a wonderful friend you were.'

I truly believe that. It hasn't taken long for me to be welcomed into the tight-knit community.

'That's very kind. We never parted in a bad way; she just moved on, I guess. I know she found it painful being in the house without your father. All the same, it would be lovely to see her.'

I hadn't really appreciated that Mum might have found the house too quiet.

We are standing outside as a group of volunteers are salting the footpaths between the graves and clearing away any ice and snow with a shovel, to make them less treacherous. Marilyn has just handed out hot drinks to the grateful workers, who take a break from their hard work.

Just then Gerard appears from the church and wraps me in a hug. I feel so happy that Marilyn and Gerard found each other. They are two of the nicest people you could ever wish to meet.

'Don't be a stranger, young Ruby,' he says, giving me one

last squeeze goodbye. It makes me smile that he still calls me young Ruby.

'I won't be,' I reply, wondering if I really mean it. 'I will do my best to return at Easter and let's hope Mum will join me.' Although I don't really hold out much hope. Mum seems to have closed the door on the chapter of her life that involved living here in Brindleford. Still, you never know. 'And I'll keep in touch, of course, as I will want to know all about the library situation,' I tell Marilyn, who gives me one final goodbye hug.

EIGHTEEN

I'd been counting down the hours until I return to London, yet now it feels strange to be leaving Brindleford today. Even though I have only been here for a short while it feels like so much longer. Perhaps it's the slower place of life. Fleetingly, I wonder if the weather will change again...

My mind drifts to Will as I cross the road towards the church to meet him. I spot him parking up and heading towards me.

'Morning! So are you all packed and ready to head home?' he asks brightly.

'I am indeed.'

We take the path that I know so well along the side of the church and are soon on open farmland.

'I've enjoyed spending time with you,' Will says as we walk. 'It's a shame you won't be here for much longer.'

He glances at me and smiles.

'I have enjoyed spending time with you too.' I return his compliment. 'And I owe you dinner – you've cooked for me twice now.'

'Strictly speaking, I was already cooking for other people, and I invited you along. Actually, that sounds bad. I would have loved to have cooked for you alone.'

'You would?'

'Of course I would. I would have got the candles out and everything.' For a second, I can imagine myself in his beautiful house, being wined and dined by candlelight and wishing I didn't have to head home.

'Well, I can at least shout you a hot chocolate from the hut you told me about.'

'Done!'

It's a beautiful morning with a bright blue sky, but with a chill in the air. The kind of morning I recall June at the Swan telling me she loves.

I listen to birdsong as we walk and spot a blackbird on the branch of a tree. Dad once told me that blackbirds and robins are amongst the many birds that do not migrate from these parts. I impart this information to Will, but he doesn't say much in response.

In the distance, I spot a cluster of trees surrounding the library building. As I imagine them being removed to make way for the new housing, I feel a surge of anger inside. I'm determined to find out the truth and resolve to ask Will when we're closer to the library.

Approaching Hope Farm, I glance over towards the cowsheds, half expecting to see a wife and maybe a farm worker tending the farm, but it is quiet as we pass by. In fact, looking further, I see that the farm appears to be devoid of animals, yet wasn't Nathan taking delivery of farm machinery?

A second barn appears to have been renovated, with a sleek-looking barn conversion in its place. I assume the four-by-four in the driveway of the house must belong to Nathan's other half.

'Penny for your thoughts?' asks Will as my mind drifts back to the past.

'What? Oh nothing really, I just remember this place.' I nod towards the farmhouse. 'In fact, it was the home of my first boyfriend,' I find myself telling him.

'So, this is kind of a trip down memory lane for you?'

'In some ways, yes, I suppose it is. I haven't been back here since I was a teenager, so I guess it is bound to bring up some emotions.'

'I can imagine. Although I don't believe in looking back,' he says without emotion. 'It's pointless. Looking ahead and having a goal is what matters. To me at least.'

I wonder what happened between Will and his ex-wife, although it is clearly something he does not dwell on.

We continue on, and before we take a path that loops back into the village, I spot the drinks van up ahead.

There are a few tables outside, one occupied by a dog walker sipping a drink. His dog, a delightful chocolate cockapoo, wags its tail and strains on its lead to say hi, so I pet the animal, but Will completely ignores it.

'Shall we?' Will gestures to a table. 'Or do you prefer to grab a takeaway and walk?'

'Actually, let's sit,' I say before I order him a coffee, and a hot chocolate for me.

'Are you not a dog lover, then?' I ask, as the dog walker finishes his coffee and moves on.

'Not especially.' He shrugs. He took little interest in the local birds too, so clearly he's not an animal lover in general. Mum always said to beware of men who don't like children or animals.

Despite the chill in the air that bites at my cheeks, and the library on my mind, I find myself beginning to relax as I walk through the countryside. There is something so soothing about engaging with nature, which, I realise, I do very little of when back in London. There was a time when I would head to the parks, but even that seems to have stopped of late. I really must try and do some more exercise, something I often think about but never seem to get around to doing.

I enjoy the crunch of the grass beneath my feet on the solid ground and the sight of the bare trees, their branches gilded with the remains of the snow. Every patch of soil or fallen twig stands out against the wintery white snow, the landscape a pretty winter wonderland.

When we eventually approach the side of the library, I decide to ask Will directly about the new houses.

'So where exactly did you say the new-builds will be?' I ask. Just then I almost slip on some icy ground and have to grab on to his arm.

'Around here, I told you,' he says as I steady myself.

'But where exactly? I did hear it may be on the site of the library and children's park.'

He attempts to walk on, but I stay put and glance at the library. It makes me mad to think about it not being here anymore.

'And what would be the problem with that?' he says without any emotion. 'The council are struggling with their budget and apparently most people don't use the library anyway.' He shrugs. 'They head off to the bigger one in the next town.'

'Well, the council would say that, wouldn't they?' I say, surprised at quite how angry I feel. 'And children need to be introduced to books at a very early age. Besides, it's not just about the books; the library hosts many other activities—'

'But building new houses will actually bring more money into the area.' Will cuts me off mid flow.

'For what exactly?' I ask. 'A new library or play area? I highly doubt it. And unless the rates are lowered on the high street rents, there will be no more shops,' I fume.

'There is actually talk of a new leisure centre being built not far from here, with a brand-new swimming pool.'

'Well, a leisure centre is unlikely to be here in the village, is it?' I reason. 'More likely in the next big town.'

'Look,' he says, turning to face me. 'The library will go anyway, so if not me, some other developer would buy up the land.' He shrugs without an ounce of guilt. 'It's hardly worth worrying about.'

Hardly worth worrying about?

'Taking a library and a kids' park from a village is not something to worry about?' I ask, wondering if he has a shred of decency in him.

'It's business,' he replies coolly. 'Besides, the council haven't exactly agreed the planning permission yet,' he reveals. 'Although I imagine it will be going full steam ahead after Christmas.'

'It is business to you, but I am sure a lot of people around here are going to feel the effects.' But deep down, I know nothing I say will make him rethink his building plans.

'Anyway, I am surprised that you are so concerned about it, as you don't even live here anymore. It's hardly the end of the world losing an under-used library, is it?

'And a kids' play area, that I am sure is very well used,' I retort. 'In fact, I know it is.'

Even in this weather, I noticed children wrapped up and playing on the swings with their families and friends.

I have often heard it said that what comes out of a person's mouth has the potential to put you off them for life, and never has there been a more perfect example of this. I suddenly feel nothing but distaste for the man walking beside me, despite his good looks. How can someone not care about changing the very heart of a village, even though the council are the ones who are ultimately responsible? One thing is for sure. They need to be stopped. Especially as the planning permission has not actually been granted yet.

'Well, I know having chatted to Marilyn that the villagers

are very much against it.' As we walk, I try to compose myself. I don't disclose the fact that I will tell Marilyn that the housing plans are still in motion. Things will need to move quickly.

'Things change,' says Will. 'If they didn't, we would still have stocks on the market square, and people bring pelted with rotten tomatoes.' He laughs at his own remark. There is someone I would not mind seeing in those stocks right now.

Passing the library and heading back towards the church, I paint on my brightest smile and thank Will for the walk this morning.

'Thanks for the drink. And it would be great if we could keep in touch,' he says, seemingly unaware that he has offended me in any way.

'Well, you have my number,' I tell him. 'Although London is a very long way from here.'

I wonder how a guy as lovely as Henry could have a son who is seemingly only concerned about money and little else.

Outside the hotel, I quickly say goodbye, as Will gives me a peck on the cheek.

'Safe journey back, then, it's been a pleasure.'

'Thanks. It's been lovely meeting you too,' I say with gritted teeth, before I head inside.

As I approach the entrance to the hotel, I suddenly find myself turning around and having one last-ditch attempt to ask Will to have a change of heart.

'Look, I know the wheels are in motion, but you will upset a lot of people if you go ahead with your building plans. Surely there is plenty more land you could have chosen?' I suggest.

'Not really,' he says matter-of-factly. 'A lot of it has a preservation order on it. People will get used to having the new houses, especially the next generation. As I said, change is inevitable.'

'So that's it, you won't consider looking elsewhere – maybe even somewhere out of town?'

'No, I'm afraid not,' he replies firmly. And in that moment, I know what I must do.

NINETEEN

I walk along the high street towards the hotel, taking things slowly as the pavements are icy, and take in every single shop that is decorated with Christmas decorations, from full-on flashing trees in the windows of some shops, to subtle silver streamers hanging down in the window of the clothes store.

The fruit and veg shop has boxes of clementines and chestnuts displayed on a table outside, alongside pretty Poinsettia plants with their striking scarlet leaves. Every single shop owner has tried to make their shops look seasonal and joyful, reminding me once more of the sense of community here.

I am almost back at the hotel and give one glance back down the high street, when suddenly I'm falling. I trip over and hear the crack almost instantly as I land on the icy pavement and scream out in pain. Just at that moment, snow begins to slowly swirl from the sky. You have to be kidding.

'Oh, my goodness, what's happened?' June is out of the door of the hotel at once, having heard me cry out. The pain sears through my body as I realise I can't put any weight onto my foot when I attempt to stand. I can also feel a pair of strong arms around me, helping me to my feet.

'Nathan,' I say in shock, breathing through the pain.

'Does it hurt?' Pippa holds her mum's hand and looks as if she is about to burst into tears. Suddenly a crowd is surrounding me. The snowflakes seem to be gathering momentum, as people throw up the hoods on their coats.

'It does,' I tell her truthfully.

'I'm sorry I dropped my dog.'

I didn't notice the child's wooden toy on the floor. It's broken in two – hopefully that was the crack I heard and not me.

'It wasn't your fault.' I smile through my pain.

'We need to get you off that cold floor, and inside,' June resolves.

'I'll call an ambulance.' Esme's face is etched with concern. Is it that bad?

'No, no really I don't think there is any need for that.' I shake my head, despite the unbearable pain shooting through my lower leg. Perhaps if I just get inside and put my feet up for a while I will be okay. It's probably nothing more than a sprain.

'I definitely think you need to get checked out at the hospital,' Nathan agrees.

Inside, June somehow manages to gently remove my boot, revealing an already swollen ankle.

She dashes off for a moment, before returning with a glass of water and some pills. 'Here, swallow down a couple of these. Take three; it will really take the edge off. I was prescribed them after my hysterectomy last year.'

At this point, I would gladly take some ketamine from a street dealer if I was offered it. I swallow down the pills gratefully, hoping they will quickly take effect.

Esme calls her paramedic husband to see if there are any ambulances in the area. 'Although I will still need to put in the emergency call,' she explains to me.

How can this be happening? Five minutes ago, I was

finishing a walk through the countryside and now here I am, hardly able to move.

'They are a little busy this morning,' Esme says after finishing a call. 'But an ambulance should be with you in around an hour.'

'We can be at the hospital in half an hour.' Nathan glances at his watch. 'I'll drive you there.'

'No, no please, I am sure you are busy today,' I protest.

'Nothing I can't cancel. I will be back for the wedding.' He turns to June, who is hosting the reception at the pub.

'Then just drop me at the hospital,' I tell Nathan. 'I will be fine from there.'

'Let's just see what happens when we get there,' he says. 'I'll bring my car to the front of the hotel.'

I am somehow carefully manoeuvred into Nathan's car, and before we arrive at the hospital, the drugs that June gave me are beginning to take effect. The pain has not completely dulled, yet I don't seem to mind it. This surreal world I find myself in, where everything feels soft around the edges, is rather pleasant. Catching my reflection in the car window, I can see myself grinning like a Cheshire cat. What on Earth did June give me, I wonder? She did tell me the name, but somehow, it's too distant for me to grasp.

Maybe it's just as well that I feel semi-comatose, as the realisation hits me that I will not be on that two o'clock train. And there is absolutely nothing I can do about it.

TWENTY

Thankfully, I don't have to wait too long before I am ushered into a cubicle in A & E.

'Have you taken anything?' the nurse asks as she wraps the cuff of a blood pressure monitor around my arm.

'What? Oh, yes just a painkiller.' I smile.

'Do you know what it was called?'

'Trapezium,' I tell her. 'No wait, trampoline. I think.'

'Tramadol?'

'I think that's it. Yes, yes it was.' I grin.

'Right,' she says, with a raise of an eyebrow. 'Well, my money is on your ankle being broken, but you will need an X-ray to confirm it. If it needs setting in plaster, you will be flying as high as a kite with the gas and air.' She looks at the numbers on the blood pressure reading. 'And taking other people's prescribed medication is never a good idea,' she tells me firmly. 'You could have reacted badly to it.'

'It will be fine.' I smile, wondering what on Earth she is worrying about. Life is good. Can I really hear birds singing?

Nathan appears then and says something to the nurse.

'I thought you were going home?' I ask him.

'No, I told you I was going to park the car, after I dropped you here.'

'Did you?'

'I did.' He smiles and exchanges a knowing look with the nurse.

'Really, you should go, you are getting married later,' I say.

The nurse gives a puzzled look.

'I am attending a wedding,' explains Nathan, and, despite my advanced stages of oblivion, I note the smile on the nurse's face.

'Oh I love a wedding. I think they bring out the romance in people.' She winks.

Is she flirting with him, whilst I am here floating about in pain? Who could blame her, though. He is *seriously* hot.

Just then, a porter appears, and I am helped into the chair to head down to the X-ray department.

'The plans are not set in stone...' I tell Nathan.

'What are you talking about?' He frowns.

'The library houses, I mean the houses on the library site. They need to be stopped!' I raise my arm in the air.

And suddenly, I have no more thoughts.

A couple of hours later, I awake to a plaster cast around my foot. I vaguely remember sucking on some gas and air, but little else after that. Thankfully, the effects of the painkillers appear to have worn off, and I feel a little more alert.

Nathan is walking towards me clutching two coffees. What on Earth is he doing here?

'You're awake,' he says, placing a coffee down on a bedside table.

'Where's Marilyn?' I feel thrown by his appearance and I can feel my face colour a little.

'So you don't remember coming here with me?'

'With you?' I ask, confused. 'I could have sworn I came in Marylin's car.'

'Well, you were a bit out of it, so I am not surprised you don't remember,' he says with the raise of an eyebrow.

'Have you been here the whole time?' I ask.

'No, I went and did a few jobs. I told you I would come back and take you to the village.'

'You did?'

'I did.' He grins.

'Well, it was kind of you to bring me here, so thank you.' I smile.

We finish our drinks, then I remember that I need to speak to Marilyn.

'I need to get out of here,' I tell him.

'Let's go.' He tosses our coffee cups into a nearby bin, and I ease myself into a standing position with the aid of a crutch, resisting his help.

'So how are you feeling?' Nathan asks once we are seated in his comfortable car.

'Not too bad.' But my heart sinks when I glance down at the boot my lower leg is encased in. It seems my ankle is broken.

'And I am sorry, but Marilyn told me to remind you that you have missed your train...' he informs me. 'Maybe it's meant to be that you are here with us for a little longer.' He turns to look at me with those brown eyes that always made my stomach flip. And still do.

Back at the hotel, Nathan drops me off and heads back to the farm.

'Oh, my dear, are you alright?' June asks with concern when she spots me. 'And I take it this means you will be needing the room for another night?'

'I guess I will, and yes, I am fine, but you never told me how strong those drugs were.'

'Oh dear, maybe I should have done.' She pulls a face. 'And perhaps three was a tad over the top, but I bet they did you some good, hey?'

'They certainly did I guess, although I wouldn't go handing them out to anyone else. The nurse ticked me off for taking someone else's medication.'

'Noted,' she says a little sheepishly. 'Anyway, I only have a couple left in case of an emergency.'

'Actually, June. Do you offer a laundry service? I am pretty much out of clothes, and I don't see a launderette on the high street.'

The one I remember as a child is now a clothing shop.

'Not strictly, love, you are not in some fancy London hotel now.' She laughs. 'But give them to me; I will put them through our washer–dryer.'

'Thank you so much, June.'

'Consider it done, hang on a sec.' She disappears before returning with a plastic bin liner. 'Just shove your things in there.'

I freshen up back in my room, thankful that I showered this morning, as it could be interesting trying to manoeuvre myself into the shower wearing this cast. I am thankful that I have a ground-floor room.

After June has taken my washing, I call Coleen.

'Oh, you are joking!' she exclaims when I tell her about my accident.

'I'm afraid not. I'll have to stay here this evening – there's actually a wedding in the church that I've been told it will be okay to attend. It will give me a chance to practise walking on these crutches.'

'On the ice?' she asks, aghast.

'Actually, there has been a fresh snowfall, so it isn't slippy.

Besides, it's only across the road and June has offered to escort me there. What else will I be doing apart from feeling sorry for myself?'

'I guess so but take it easy. I hope you're back here for Christmas Day... Now you have even more reason to be waited on hand and foot.'

'Thanks, Coleen. That's really kind. I will keep you updated this end,' I assure her.

'Goodbye, my friend, take care.'

TWENTY-ONE

A few hours later, June has returned my laundry and I'm dressed and ready for the wedding. There's a tap on my door and I open it to see her looking pretty in a pale pink dress, and an oyster-coloured faux fur bolero. Next to her is her husband, Joe, who I've never met as he spends so much time in the kitchen, and we're introduced for the first time.

'Are you ready, hun?' June asks.

'I am, although I don't really feel dressed for a wedding...' I am wearing my trusty black trousers and a blue blouse I had packed and not yet worn.

I had considered not bothering going to the church service, but what else would I be doing other than sitting here with my feet up? Besides, it's true, I want to get on them and become accustomed to using the crutches.

Outside, I walk carefully with June beside me, and soon enough I am taking a seat in the beautifully decorated church. The interior takes my breath away as I take in the stunning flower displays and the cream candles gently flickering at the front of the church.

The violin quartet playing at the front of the church

suddenly changes to the traditional wedding march and Marilyn slides into the seat on the other side of me.

'Are you okay?' she whispers.

'Fine. It's a distraction being here – it might stop me from crying in my room.' She gives my arm a little squeeze in response.

There are collective gasps as the beautiful bride slowly makes her way down the aisle. The man I assume to be her father cannot keep the smile from his face as he escorts her to her awaiting groom. I feel a punch to the heart when I realise it is something my father will never be able to do for me, should I ever marry.

As the ceremony is about to begin in front of the packed-out church, I glance around, and my eyes fall on Nathan. I feel my mouth go dry and my heart beat that little bit faster. He locks eyes with me and smiles, and my pulse rate goes through the roof.

TWENTY-TWO

I resist the urge to turn around again as I watch the beautiful wedding ceremony unfold in front of the altar with the flickering candles.

The bride is wearing a simple long white satin gown, and her long blonde hair is threaded with winter flowers. The groom is wearing a rather fetching lilac checked suit, and open-necked white shirt with a large purple flower in the buttonhole.

I can't help but think that this is the place I would probably have got married to Nathan. I wonder if he married his wife here. It seems more than likely that he would, and the thought of it makes me feel a little empty.

When Gerard finishes the service and the couple are declared man and wife, he takes the opportunity to tell the congregation how wonderful it is to see us all here and reminds us about midnight mass on Christmas Eve.

The couple, both smiling and looking very much in love, walk back up the aisle to the strains of a beautiful love song by a well-known artist.

As Marilyn heads outside to congratulate the couple, I spot

Nathan making his way towards me and I feel myself go a little lightheaded.

'We will have to stop meeting like this!' He grins.

He looks even more handsome – if that were possible – dressed in a smart navy suit. In a certain light, I notice how his dark hair is lightly peppered with grey at the sides, which only seems to enhance his looks. It would appear Nathan is one of those guys that gets better looking as they age.

'I know, people will talk.' I smile, trying to stop myself from looking into his eyes.

'So how long will you be staying on?'

'For tonight at least. I hope to finally get away tomorrow,' I tell him.

'That's nice.' He smiles that gorgeous smile. 'I mean that you will be staying on tonight. Maybe we can have that catch-up later, then?'

Nathan picks up my crutches from the floor, before taking me by the hand and helping me up.

The touch of his hand in mine gives me those butterflies again, but I push the feelings away. Especially knowing that he has a wife and two children – even though he appears to be on his own today.

'So, see you back at the Swan Inn for the reception, then?' he asks as I steady myself onto my crutches, hardly able to believe that I am here in Brindleford chatting to my first love.

'Um not really, I just came to watch the wedding. I am not exactly a guest...'

'You know me, though.' He grins. 'And you can be my plus-one if you like, as my original one has let me down. Look, I know I aways seem to be dashing off somewhere, but I have to take delivery of something at the farm. I'll be back in half an hour. And don't worry, I'll square you joining with my friend – he's the groom.'

I am about to ask him who his original plus-one was. Surely it would have been his wife. And where are the children?

Feeling a little confused at where his wife and children are, and who his original plus-one was, I make my way outside, as a photographer is asking a group to get together for a picture. I notice Nathan jump in for the picture and smile broadly, before he darts off, waving to me as he leaves.

What is going on here? I need to ask Marilyn and find out, but she is busy elsewhere. Just then, June appears and links her arm through mine.

'So are you coming to the wedding reception?'

'I'm not really invited,' I remind her. 'Although Nathan did say I could be his plus-one.'

'Well, there you are, then. I would have sorted something anyway. We can't have you sitting in your room alone all evening, can we?'

'Don't worry about me I...'

'June, June! Come on, you need to get in this photo.' The bride is gesturing her towards the group ready to be photographed.

'Speak later,' June says as she dashes off.

Whilst the photos are being taken, I decide to carefully make my way back to the hotel.

Back in my room, I wonder what it was that I felt when Nathan took my hand and helped me up from the pew in church. Do I really want to see him later, as his plus-one, and unearth a load of old feelings? Perhaps I ought to stay here holed up in my room until I can leave tomorrow. I still haven't watched those Christmas movies I promised myself I would...

I am sitting daydreaming and wondering whether I ought to call Mum, when I get a text from Sienna from the studio.

Hi Ruby, how are you doing?

I'd sent her a picture of my leg in plaster whilst I was in the hospital and it's nice that she's checking in on me. I decide to give her a call.

'Hi, Sienna, not too bad thanks. Hopefully I'll be on my way home tomorrow.'

'Oh that's good. I can't believe you have broken your ankle, you poor thing,' she says sympathetically.

'I know, no ice skating for me this Christmas.'

'So the trains are up and running then?'

'Fingers crossed they will be,' I tell her. 'I was actually going to call you later and ask you if I am right in thinking Amanda Lewis is currently working for Yorkshire TV?'

'I believe so, yes. Some sort of roving reporter, although the poor girls seem to get sent out in all weathers, reporting on all manner of things. Flooded streets, missing dogs on the moors, anything that requires her standing around and freezing half to death apparently.'

Sienna made friends with Amanda after she covered me in my absence and has stayed in touch.

'I guess we all have to start somewhere,' I say, thinking of the days I would be reviewing a market stall café, or similar.

'We do indeed, anyway, so why do you ask?'

'I was just thinking there might be a story she would be interested in covering, right here in Brindleford.'

I tell her all about the possible library closure.

'That's awful. And actually, I think that is something she probably would like to be involved in; I will text her number to you.'

'Thanks, Sienna, speak to you soon.'

I make myself a cup of tea, and half an hour later, there is a knock on my bedroom door. It's probably June coming to take me downstairs to a wedding reception that I feel entirely inappropriately dressed for. Perhaps I will stay here and watch a movie after all.

Opening the bedroom door, I am preparing myself to tell June I will skip the wedding meal, when I see Nathan standing in front of me.

'Nathan, hi!'

'So, are you coming to the meal as my guest, or what?' he asks.

'I'm not sure... I'm hardly dressed for a wedding, and there will definitely be no dancing,' I say and his face breaks into a smile. That gorgeous smile.

'Firstly, you look beautiful as you are,' he says, locking eyes with me. 'Secondly, maybe you could manage a slow dance later. You could hold on to me,' he offers, and the thought of being in his arms almost makes me fall off my crutches. 'Oh, and thirdly, who is going to eat your wedding meal? You don't want your venison going to waste, do you? Or the poor deer will have died in vain.'

'Hardly, as there are plenty of other guests.' I raise an eyebrow. 'Anyway, I'm still not sure about coming; it feels like an intrusion.'

'Come for the meal at least,' he suggests. 'It's a celebration, the more the merrier. You remember how things work around here?'

'I do, of course.'

'Then please, join me. It will give us a chance to have that much-needed catch-up. I want to hear all about your life in London,' he says persuasively.

June appears and hurries us along. Although hurry is hardly the word, in my case. 'Come on, you two. Hubby tells me the staff are about to serve the meal.'

She ushers us towards the dining room that looks resplendent and not a bit like the breakfast room I dined in this morning.

The low oak beams have dried flowers hanging from them and the stone walls have lit candle sconces. The tables are set with white flower displays, courtesy of the talented ladies from the church who are also guests.

We are shown to our table, that I am pleased to see, includes Marilyn and Gerard and another couple, who smile and introduce themselves.

'I asked another couple from the village if they would mind moving tables, so we could sit together,' explains Marilyn.

Just then a waitress appears and sets down glasses of champagne in preparation for a toast.

'Thank you, that's great, although I still feel a bit like an imposition,' I say to Marilyn.

'Nonsense.' She smiles. 'They were perfectly happy to swap.'

She nods towards the couple who are chatting and laughing at something the couple next to them have said.

I am about to ask Nathan about why he is here alone, when someone taps a spoon against a glass ready to make an announcement.

The bride's father welcomes everyone to the wedding and thanks them for coming. He gives a charming speech before we are all asked to raise our glasses in a toast to the bride and groom.

I watch the bride and groom at the front table, flanked by both sets of parents and once more think of how my dad won't be present at my wedding, should I ever have one. Come to think of it, will my mum? I am pretty sure she would, assuming she's still around, which is a depressing thought.

Our first course of a delicious farmhouse pâté is served, which Nathan tells me was supplied by his very own farm.

'You sell produce?'

'I have a farm shop,' he says as he spreads the pâté onto a

thin slice of toast. 'Which I am happy to say is proving to be very popular.'

'So, you don't have Hope Farm anymore?' I ask, recalling there was no sign of a shop when I walked past it yesterday morning.

'No,' he tells me as he pours me some wine from a bottle.

'What happened?' I ask. 'I imagined you taking over the place, having been brought up learning the trade.'

'Oh, I did for a while,' he explains as he takes a sip of his champagne. 'But I sold up after the divorce.'

TWENTY-THREE

'You're divorced?'

I put down my glass of wine as I take in the news and I wonder why I feel something in the pit of my stomach.

'I am. Four years ago now. After we divorced, I sold up and bought a farmhouse and some land to grow vegetables. Over the last few years, we have steadily built up the business to include a farm shop. We even have a cottage to rent along with a few glamping pods,' he says. 'Things are going really well.'

'Wow that sounds amazing, so no animals then?'

'Chickens – we sell the eggs in the shop – and a few goats and a couple of pigs. Families like to visit, and the kids love the animals, along with the wooden adventure playground.' He paints a picture of quite the local attraction.

'Ah right. So, when you say *we* have built up the business...?'

'Me and Dad. He lives in a cottage on the land. He is game-keeper and general caretaker. Sadly, Mum is with us no more.'

'Oh, I am so sorry, Nathan. I always liked your mum,' I say sincerely.

'Thanks. It's been two years now. I don't think Dad would

still be around if he didn't have his projects helping around the farm. Well, imparting his wisdom mainly, but the young workers don't seem to mind.'

'It all sounds amazing.'

'Thanks. It's been a labour of love, but I have enjoyed it. I realised the locals might enjoy having a farm shop, but people drive for miles for the produce, which is also used in the onsite café. You should come and see it whilst you are here,' he suggests. 'It was even featured on an episode of *Yorkshire Farming* once.'

'That's brilliant – and maybe I will. So, do you have a family?' I ask. 'To be honest, I was wondering why you were alone here today.'

'I do. Twin boys, Dylan and Joe.' He smiles at the mention of their names.

'I assume they are with their mother?' I ask, hoping I am not prying too much.

'No, they are both at university,' he tells me as he slices into his venison. 'They will both be arriving home to spend Christmas with me. They alternate Christmas with me and their mother, although they are adults now. As Leanne is away this year, I'm pleased to have my boys stay with me.'

I don't recognise the name Leanne as someone from the village, but I guess they could have met anywhere.

'Your sons are at university?' I ask, completely surprised. Didn't Phylis tell me that Nathan had little boys?

'That's right, Dylan is studying business management, and Joe is studying to be a vet. They were keen to spread their wings, but they are always around in the holidays.'

A waitress appears at the table offering more wine and I accept a glass of red. The man on the other side of Nathan begins a conversation with him then, leaving me thinking about how Nathan is now divorced with grown-up sons.

His boys are at university, I think to myself as I reapply

some lipstick in the bathroom mirror. So for a lot of the year, he is alone at the farm. Well, apart from with his father and staff. It would be nice to see to see his dad; he was a nice man, if a little forthright in his opinions as I recall.

As the wedding meal draws to a close, people are sitting around chatting in lounge chairs and a team of workers clear the tables and line them up against a wall, where a buffet will appear later this evening.

'Are you okay?' Nathan has noticed me suppress a yawn.

'I guess I am a little tired… It's been a long day, and this ankle is a bit of a drag, literally.'

'We could take a drink to your room, if you like?'

'Hmmm, I'm not sure,' I say uncertainly.

'Sorry,' says Nathan, holding his hands up. 'That was a crass thing to say, suggesting going to your room. I hope you know that I wasn't going to suggest anything improper,' he adds emphatically.

'I am sure you weren't.' I smile. 'But I think I will go for a lie-down anyway. I hardly slept a wink last night.'

'Then let me at least escort you to your room.'

'Sure.'

Nathan walks me to my room and when I open the door, I decide to invite him inside anyway.

'Maybe if you are going to continue partying, you could do with a coffee,' I suggest.

'I'd like that.'

Sitting with our drinks, Nathan on a wing-backed chair, me on the window seat, I tell him about my encounter with Phylis.

'Poor Phylis is confused,' he tells me. 'She has recently been diagnosed with dementia, but I'm told her memory is deteriorating pretty quickly.'

'That must be awful for her.'

'It must be. I remember when she had the Greyhound pub and how she loved to chat to the customers.'

'Me too. And us trying to get served when we were under-age.' We both laugh.

'And those long snogs in the alleyway on the walk home.'

His comment gives me tingles throughout my body as those heady days come rushing back. We would have picnics in fields in the summer months, and strolls along country paths that would often end in passionate encounters in the barn, yet never quite fully having sex.

I'm not sure what really held me back, but maybe deep down I was trying to protect my own feelings as well as Nathan's, knowing I wasn't going to be staying around.

Plus, living in a small village and attending the doctor's for contraception at the age of seventeen was something I didn't fancy doing either, so the risk of getting pregnant was always there in the back of mind. If I close my eyes, I can picture us locked in an embrace, Nathan breathing heavily and telling me how much I drove him crazy with desire.

'Phylis told me you had little boys.' I'm keen to change the subject of our teenage years, as I feel the heat rise in my cheeks. 'I thought you had only been married a few years.'

'Quite the opposite,' he says, placing his coffee cup down. 'I met Leanne a year after you left and was married the following year.

It seems Nathan moved on pretty quickly.

'I see.'

Nathan's phone rings then, and he answers. 'I'll be there in a minute; no, I haven't gone home,' he says with an eye roll. 'See you in a bit.

'You are sure you won't join me for that slow dance later?' he asks, as he sits next to me on the window seat, our arms touching in the small space. He smells good enough to eat.

'I can't make any promises. I'll probably be fast asleep in an hour.'

'Then can I see you tomorrow? I would love to show you around the farm.'

'I am hoping to be on my way back to London then...'

'Do you really need to leave tomorrow?' He searches my eyes, and I wish he would stand and put a little distance between us.

Do I need to? I ask myself. And will a day really make any difference?

'Perhaps I could stay.' I shrug. 'But I will have to check about keeping the room. I am sure June said something about people booking in over the Christmas holidays.'

'Maybe I can help with that,' he replies, finally standing and moving towards the door. 'So, can I see you tomorrow?' he asks once more, as I see him out.

He looks so handsome standing in the open doorway, his arm resting on the door frame, the collar of his shirt open, his tie now discarded. I take in his eternally handsome face and dark hair and find myself agreeing.

'Okay. You can collect me at eleven if that suits?' I find myself saying.

'It does.' He smiles. 'It really is so good to see you, Ruby.' He gives me a peck on the cheek, and the scent of him has my pulse racing, even after all these years. I almost wish his lips would land on mine, but they don't.

As I close the door behind me, I feel filled with confusion. They do say never go back. So what exactly am I doing, delighting in the fact that Nathan is divorced, and already looking forward to seeing him again?

TWENTY-FOUR

'I am afraid I have some bad news,' Marilyn tells me when she calls the following morning. 'Planning permission has been passed for the houses. It seems the library will be no more.'

'What? I don't believe it! It was only the other day that Will told me things were still in progress...' I reply.

'Well, I am afraid it's true.' She sighs. 'Maybe the council decided to rush things through before Christmas, who knows? Perhaps Will chased it up. All I know is that the project has been okayed. And it was as I thought: apparently the proposed plans had been secured to a tree near the church. The council claim it must have been blow away or something. I mean, really...' she says in frustration.

'But surely the plans can be challenged? In fact, I'll contact my colleague at the news station. It is time to stage a protest.'

'Do you think there is any point?' she asks doubtfully. 'Because I have a feeling that only the person who has lodged the planning application has the right to appeal if it has been *declined.*'

'We have to try – there's nothing to lose,' I tell her, realising how much I want to support the library.

'Yes, yes. You are right. Perhaps the protest will whip up some local support.'

'That's the spirit!' I say, feeling positive. 'We can't give up now.'

It seems to be a morning for calls, because not long after I say goodbye to Marilyn, my phone buzzes.

'Are you telling me you aren't coming home for Christmas?' asks Coleen after I tell her about everything that's happened.

'I'm not sure I am... I have things to do here.'

'What things?' She laughs.

'Well, you know the library thing I was telling you about? It turns out the planning permission has just been agreed. We need to be full steam ahead with protests and I'm hoping regional news will cover it on television. Marilyn has launched an online petition that already has a thousand signatures!'

'So where will you stay?' she asks. 'It's entirely your decision of course, but do you really want to be spending Christmas Day in a hotel?'

'I have been offered an alternative actually,' I reply, wondering whether I am actually considering Nathan's offer, that is metres away from his farmhouse where he lives with his dad.

As I prepare to tell Coleen about running into Nathan, I can feel my fingers tingle with excitement.

'I ran into my first love the other day...' I tell her, hardly able to believe what I am saying.

I had told Coleen all about Nathan during one of our many girly film and wine evenings at her place when her hubby was out and we had discussed our first loves.

'Nathan? You're kidding! Tell me everything, what did he look like?' she asks excitedly.

'No different, in fact more handsome if anything. Gorgeous

in fact.' I let out a sigh as I think of him. 'Why do some men get better looking with age?'

'I don't know, it's hardly fair, is it? So is he married?'

'Divorced.'

'Oh my goodness. Hang on a minute. Let me switch on the camera.'

A few seconds later, I am staring at Coleen's face in her house, a row of pretty dresses on a rail behind her.

'Fancy running into Nathan, although I guess there was always the chance of that, him living in the village...' she reasons.

'I suppose so. He has sold up the old dairy farm and now runs a crop farm complete with shop, children's park, and accommodation. He's invited me over to see the farm tomorrow.'

'So, is he offering you the holiday accommodation?'

'I'm guessing so; I guess all will be revealed tomorrow.'

'How exciting. So, was there still a little bit of a spark?' she asks with a big grin on her face.

More like a burning fire, if I am honest with myself. 'I think there was, yes,' I tell her, maybe not wanting to fully admit it to myself. 'It was as if I had only seen him recently, as the years just seemed to roll back,' I say, recalling our first meeting outside the hotel.

'They say you never forget your first love, although I am more than happy to mine,' says Coleen, pulling a face.

It is hardly surprising really, as the boy she thought would love her forever left to join the army at seventeen without a backward glance and a shrug, telling her he never thought they were serious and that they were too young to be tied down.

'He did me a favour really, although it took me a long time to realise that,' she admits. 'He was right, though; we were too young to settle down.'

'Well, I do believe everything happens for a reason,' I say firmly. 'Some things are definitely meant to be.'

'Like you running into Nathan?' she asks.

'Who knows? Oh Coleen, I wish I had never had this stupid accident and been laid up here...' I sigh. 'Everything seems to make sense in London.'

'Does it?'

'I think so. I mean, I have my work and my gorgeous flat. And you of course.'

She blows me a kiss.

'I was completely content with my life.'

'Were you? You did hint from time to time that you miss being in a relationship...'

'Well, yes maybe, and I would love to see a little more of Mum, but no one's life is perfect. Overall, though, I was happy with my lot.'

'And now?' she asks, always one to get to the heart of the matter.

'I don't know...' I sigh. 'Seeing Nathan has made me question everything but even if we rekindled something, it could never work between us; our lives are so different now.'

'Oh Ruby, it sounds like you have really made a connection.'

'I don't know what I think. If he was happily married, then I wouldn't be giving us a second thought.'

'But having discovered he is divorced?'

'I'm not sure. Anyway. I'm sure things will work themselves out.' But I am not sure how.

'Because everything happens for a reason, remember.'

'Exactly.'

When we finish talking, I sit on the window seat and look out across the street, once more admiring the shops and their decorated windows. I think of the accident outside the hotel, and how it has changed everything.

The one-day train strike is long over, and glancing at my

train app on my phone, I could be heading home today if I wanted to. I tell myself that I'm simply intrigued to see what Nathan has built up over the years, but the fact is, I can't wait to see him again. There is also the small matter of supporting the locals of this village to keep their library open.

An hour later, I decide to go to the reception after all, so I slowly make my way along the corridor. Disco lights are flashing along the wooden dance floor in the dining room, and a cheesy Christmas song is playing, as children and adults alike are happily dancing away.

I glance around the room looking for Nathan, and when my eyes fall on him, he is sitting at a table having a conversation with an attractive woman, who looks maybe in her thirties.

'Ruby, you made it!' he exclaims, standing to greet me. If looks could kill, the woman at the table would have been responsible for my immediate demise.

'I did. Sorry, I don't want to disturb you,' I say, nodding to the woman who looks younger than I first thought.

'Don't be silly, let me get you a drink,' he insists, as he heads to the bar.

The woman at the table gathers her flouncy dress into her hands, and wanders off somewhere, without even saying a word.

'Gosh, what's up with her?' I ask when Nathan returns with a bottle of wine and two glasses.

'No idea.' Nathan laughs. 'She is one of the bridesmaids. We were chatting about her returning to college to study make-up. She wants to be a wedding make-up artist,' he tells me as he pours the wine.

'I bet you were riveted.' I roll my eyes.

'I like to hear about people's ambitions,' he tells me. 'Although she lost me a bit when she was talking about the importance of primer. I thought that was something you put on walls.' He laughs.

Glancing around, I can see the young woman, who is now talking to a group of people, casting glances our way.

'Maybe she read more into your interest – she keeps looking this way.'

'Forget it, although I hope I didn't give her the wrong idea,' he says, frowning. 'Anyway, she is far too young for me.' He laughs away any suggestion of something between them.

As the evening draws to a close, the bride and groom slide along the dance floor to a slow number. After a minute or two, other couples have joined them, wrapped in each other's arms, swaying to the music.

'Shall we?' says Nathan, holding his hand out.

'I don't want to risk it – I don't want anything else to get broken.'

'I wouldn't want to be responsible for that,' he tells me, and I wonder if he knows I'm not just talking about my bones.

When it is time to head back to my room, Nathan offers to escort me there.

'Sure,' I say, although I don't plan on inviting him in as I did earlier. I can feel the effects of the wine and think it's time to get some sleep. Besides, I honestly don't know if I could control myself if he tried to kiss me.

'See you tomorrow, Nathan, thanks for this evening.'

'The pleasure was all mine,' he says as he leans in and kisses me on the cheek. 'Goodnight, Ruby.'

TWENTY-FIVE

'Be careful out there!' June says as she spots me heading towards the doorway. 'The snow has all but melted, but it's still slushy underfoot.'

'Thanks, June, I promise I'll take it slowly!' I reply as I head outside. 'I have to get used to using these crutches.'

It's time to shop local and support the fashion store at the end of the high street too, I think.

Christmas tunes are playing in the background as I carefully walk into the small shop. The owner greets me, before I make my way around the rails and admire the clothes. *How are they charging these prices?* I think to myself, as I run my hands over a long, patterned dress that would cost more than twice the price in London.

A short while later, I've decided to purchase the dress, a pair of jeans and two colourful chunky sweaters. I also select a couple of T-shirts and a zip-up hoody, thinking that my silky blouses and dry-clean-only trousers are not quite the thing to wear at a farm. Noticing my injury, the kindly shop worker carries my haul of clothes to the till as I quickly call Marilyn to ask her a favour.

I pay the grateful shop owner, and my stomach is already turning over at the thought of meeting Nathan later. Even though I had planned to head off to London this morning, curiosity would have got the better of me. I am keen to see what Nathan has done with his new farm.

'Here, let me get that for you,' says the shop lady, opening the door for me just as Marilyn arrives outside. Thankfully, she was available to help me carry my shopping to the hotel.

'Good morning!' She beams and eyes the bag. 'Successful shopping trip, then?'

'Brilliant. I managed to buy some lovely things at great prices too.'

'One advantage of not living in a big city – city shop rental costs go straight on the price of the clothes I guess.'

'True. Gosh, things really have changed around here – the shop had some really gorgeous things,' I say to Marilyn as she kindly takes my bags, and I grab on to my crutches.

'I suppose Brindleford has changed quite a bit over the years... Maybe that's the reason why more young families are choosing to stay put and raise children here.'

'So, you think the new-builds are a good idea, apart from the proposed site for the latest ones, obviously?'

'I do. But they most definitely need a library and a play park, so we will press on with the protest, for all the good it will do. Oh, and I forgot to mention, it's the Victorian Christmas market on Saturday. Will you still be here?' asks Marilyn.

'That still takes place?' I ask, recalling the charming market that used to attract visitors from miles around.

'It does. I don't think it will ever stop, at least I hope not. I know it doesn't have as many stalls as the one at Skipton, but I would say it is just as enchanting.'

'I think it being smaller is part of the charm,' I say, recalling the locals standing around drinking mulled wine and chatting.

A church choir would stand beneath the clock tower in the centre, singing carols dressed in Victorian outfits.

'I'm told there will be Christmas trees for sales this year.'

I immediately think of a Christmas film and wonder whether there will be a hunk wearing a checked shirt in attendance carrying trees for grateful women.

'Thank you so much, Marilyn,' I tell her as she deposits my clothes onto the bed in my hotel room. 'I'm going to try and have a shower, with one leg outside of the cubicle.'

'I would offer to assist, but I think that might be going a step too far.' She laughs.

As I sort myself out, I think of how Mum is missing out on having a friend like Marilyn. When Mum and Dad used to have parties at ours, Marilyn would bake the most delicious cakes and pies for everyone to enjoy. Occasionally, she would bring a bottle of homebrew rhubarb wine, that I remember her and Mum drinking from teacups in the kitchen. With hindsight, maybe they were trying to hide it from Dad, knowing his liking for alcohol. It makes me realise how little we know about our childhood, apart from the parts we are allowed to observe.

Perhaps when Mum is tired of travelling and has learned to live without my father, she might decide to return here and pick up her friendship with Marilyn, who I think would like nothing more. Or maybe even move close to me in London. But I won't hold my breath on that one.

An hour later, and having successfully manged to freshen up, I head out to reception to meet Nathan, who is seated on a lounge chair sipping a coffee and chatting to a waitress.

'You're here already?' I say, wondering why he didn't let me know he had arrived.

'I arrived early, so thought I would wait here... I wouldn't have wanted to rush you,' he says, glancing down at my ankle. 'So I thought I would grab a coffee.'

Even dressed in jeans and a weatherproof jacket, he still

looks handsome, something that does not appear to have gone unnoticed by the waitress, who keeps casting glances his way as she sets a table in the dining room.

'I suppose so.' I smile. 'Although I am getting rather used to wearing this cast now.'

'Ready, then?' He stands, and the waitress looks me up and down as we head for the door.

'So how far is the farm?' I ask, once I am seated inside his comfortable four-by-four.

'Literally a minute's drive. It is probably only a ten-minute walk, but in your current state...' He laughs, glancing at the cast on my leg.

Plus, it's pretty cold this morning so I don't fancy limping along *and* freezing half to death.

I am just beginning to enjoy the warmth from the heated seats when a minute or two later, we are pulling into a large gravel driveway.

Stepping outside, I take in several large buildings – one of them clearly the farm produce shop – surrounding a large gravel courtyard.

Nathan points to a large green barn a little further along a dirt track that was once a cowshed, and he tells me is currently unused. 'I've been considering what to do with it... The other barn next door is a kind of food factory, where the vegetables are prepared for sale in the shop,' he explains. 'The produce is also used in the all-important café. I can vouch for the winter vegetable soup, the veg all grown by yours truly.' He smiles. 'We can grab some lunch in a bit if you like?'

'Yes, I'd like that,' I say, realising I skipped breakfast after going shopping early this morning, then taking a shower.

He shows me around the wonderful shop, which has a huge Christmas tree inside the entrance. Inside, the cavernous shop is filled with all manner of foodie treats, including an impressive cheese counter.

'We are lucky enough to have some brilliant local suppliers,' says Nathan, lifting a jar of local honey from a shelf. 'I did toy with the idea of keeping bees but decided against it. I thought it might take up too much time.'

Just as we are heading outside, an attractive woman around Nathan's age approaches and asks him if he is free later to sample some of the new wines.

He makes a brief introduction, before scratching his ear, and saying he will text her later.

'Is that business or pleasure?' I ask him when she leaves. 'Trying the wine, I mean.'

He takes a second before he answers. 'It depends on how you define that.' He grins. 'Business, as in sampling new stock, but there is no denying it is a pleasurable activity.'

I resist the urge to ask him what that is supposed to mean and quickly push away the image of him sharing a bottle of wine with an attractive woman. We have only just reunited after all.

After climbing into his jeep once more, Nathan shows me the glamping pods complete with a BBQ area, before heading back towards the shop, passing a huge wooden adventure playground en route.

'Wow, well, you certainly have an impressive set-up,' I compliment him. 'It seems you have thought of just about everything.'

'I like to think so.' He smiles. 'Including this.'

We have stopped outside a cute cottage with a sage-coloured front door and its own small front garden.

'I told you I could help you out if you decided to stay,' he says, moving closer and looking into my eyes. 'The cottage is for rent, and we have had a last-minute cancellation,' he informs me as he lifts a key from his pocket. 'Shall we?'

'You are telling me I can stay here?' I ask, and my heart seems to skip a beat.

'Why not? It makes perfect sense.'

None of this makes sense, I think to myself as he lets us into the cottage. Especially the feelings I have when I am around him; yet he is giving nothing away himself. He is simply being practical. Helping me out in the situation I find myself in. I tell myself to get a grip.

We step inside the charming cottage, furnished with two comfy-looking fabric sofas, either side of a wooden coffee table. A red rug sits in front of a log burner that is glowing warmly.

I glance around the cosy lounge.

'You can stay here until you decide to head back to London,' says Nathan. 'Or for as long as you like. I would love it if you could hang around for a bit longer. We have so much to talk about.'

We stand facing each other, and my heart thuds when I think he is going to move in for a kiss but suddenly, I am startled by the shrieking of a bird that has flown in through an open window. It is now sitting perched on the top of a bookshelf.

'Damn, I had forgotten I had opened the window to air the place a little!' says Nathan, bending to pick up a vase that is thankfully unbroken from the floor. After closing the window, he opens the front door and the blackbird flies out.

As I steady my breathing, I pull myself together and wonder what on Earth is going on here. Should I stay on here for Christmas and see how things work out? I can certainly write my weekly column from here, which I had planned to do later today. Or do I return to London at once, and avoid the possibility of having my heart broken for a second time? The worried thoughts swirl around in my head.

'I think I had better head back to the hotel now,' I say, feeling overwhelmed.

'Now? But we haven't had lunch yet,' he replies, a puzzled look on his face.

'I know, but I've developed a bit of a headache,' I explain as I rub my temples.

'That's a shame. But I understand if you don't feel up to it. I was looking forward to having lunch with you, though. Dad will be back from a job soon – I thought you could say hi.'

'I would have loved that, but maybe another time.' Am I really here with my first love, and about to meet his father too? Suddenly it all feels a little too much.

'Of course.' He nods. 'So, can I get you anything? Some water, painkillers maybe?' he offers.

'No really, I probably just need to lie down. I need to start work on my column for the magazine later anyway.'

'Sure. I'll take you back if that's what you want,' he says, looking a little dejected.

When he drops me off a couple of minutes later, he touches my arm as I am about to get out of the car.

'Ruby, is everything okay? Did I do something to upset you?' he asks.

The touch of his hand sets my arm hairs on end. 'No, Nathan, it's not you, it's me... Gosh, that sounds like a cliché, doesn't it,' I say with an eye roll. 'What I mean is, you have done nothing wrong. I just have a headache, then I have things to be getting on with,' I explain, as brightly as I can.

'Will you give some thought to staying in the cottage?' he asks. 'I would love us to spend some more time together. I still haven't heard about your life in London,' he reminds me.

'I will do.' I smile. 'But the truth is, I don't know how long I will be staying here. I have a restaurant review on Christmas Eve, so I will need to return for that.'

And once I'm back in London, I am not sure I will ever return to Brindleford.

TWENTY-SIX

'I heard you were still here.' Will Sutton approaches with me a broad grin as I make my way into the hotel.

'Will, hi!' I force a smile. It's hard not to smile, really. Will is undeniably attractive, if totally money motivated. But then, maybe most businessmen are. Perhaps Nathan was ruthless in his negotiations for the site of his farm business, for all I know. I suddenly damn this place and the uncertainty it has presented in my life.

'How did you hear?' I ask, thinking that he doesn't actually live in Brindleford.

'From a mutual friend of mine and Nathan's,' he tells me. 'She works for him on his farm. It's quite the place he has there.'

'It is,' I agree. 'And a friend, you say?'

'Well, I say that, but I think she is more Nathan's on-off girl-friend,' he divulges. 'It seems Nathan hasn't really settled with anyone since his divorce.'

'Not that it's anyone else's business,' I reply.

'You're right, it isn't.' He shrugs. 'I think she just has a bit of a thing for him, but she says he prefers to play the field these days.'

'Again, that is no one's business,' I say, despite the news having my heart sink.

'I guess not.' He looks me in the eyes. 'But as you did tell me he was an ex, maybe you ought to know what he is like.'

'Because?

'I don't know, maybe in case you become reacquainted. I am just giving you a heads-up, that's all... I like you, Ruby, and I wouldn't like to see you getting hurt.'

I wonder whether he is being genuine. Why would he not be?

'Thanks for your concern, Will, but you don't need to worry about me.' I give a small smile.

'Good to know. So do you fancy a coffee?' He gestures to the nearby book café.

'I'll pass on this occasion, thanks; I have a bit of a headache.' Ultimately, I can't forgive him for the proposed demolition of the library and play park, no matter how sexy he is.

'No problem. See you around!'

As he wanders off, at exactly the same time we both turn around to check each other out, and Will gives a sidelong grin. The quicker I get inside and pour myself a large gin, the better.

I move the small dressing table to face the window, where I set up my laptop, before I pour myself a large drink.

Dark clouds have appeared outside, suddenly obscuring the previous sunshine, and seeming to match my mood perfectly, as I prepare to write my article.

As I take in Roberto's and observe one or two people entering for lunch, I think back to my evening there and can almost taste the mouth-watering food.

I sink my teeth into the delicious tart that tastes absolutely divine.

My writing comes easily, as I tell readers about my time here in Brindleford, and the charming high street. I mention the cosy eighteenth-century Swann Inn where I've been staying and of course the wonderful food on offer at Roberto's, along with the local walks he suggested I make readers aware of, including one or two of my own personal favourite strolls. I also talk about the surprisingly good clothes store, and how it sells fashionable pieces at a great price.

A couple of hours later, I've fired off my article to the magazine editor and flicked on the television to find a Christmas movie is playing. An impossibly handsome guy is flirting with a customer at a coffee shop, where she works as a barista, and I roll my eyes before flicking over to a different channel.

I settle on a house renovation programme, where two muscular men are knocking down a wall with sledgehammers. It would appear I cannot escape alpha males today, so I switch channels again and find a nature programme, featuring a snowy landscape and some robins eating from a bird feeder. Perfect.

Nursing my drink, I think about the events of the day, and consider Will's comments. Surely Nathan doesn't have a reputation as a ladies' man? Then again, what do I really know about him? After all, it has been half a lifetime since we were romantically involved. Perhaps he is just having some fun following his divorce... which neither I, nor anyone else has any right to judge him for.

Come to think of it, though, the woman at the farm did seem rather keen to enjoy some wine with him... and the young woman at the wedding was certainly captivated by him.

I sip my drink and think about the moment he was about to kiss me in the cottage. How easy it would have been to have gone along with it, had there been no interruption. And then what? An intimate liaison then goodbye from him without a backward glance?

If anything is going to distract me from those thoughts, it's getting involved with something I promised I would try and help with. I take out my phone and find the number for Amanda Lewis and dial her number.

'Amanda, hi, it's Ruby Holmes. Do you have a minute to talk?'

'Local TV news are coming here tomorrow?' asks a shocked Marilyn when I impart the news to her later.

'Yep. One o'clock sharp. I know it's short notice, but long enough to get some protestors with banners together, I hope.'

'Of course!' she says. 'Oh Ruby, how wonderful! Maybe Gerard could do a little promo of the church too, inviting people to come along to our services.'

'Maybe, although I think we should concentrate on the matter in hand...'

'Yes, yes of course, what am I like.' She laughs. 'Even though I believe you should never miss an opportunity in life.' She winks. 'At least the church will be in the camera shot, at least I hope so,' she says.

'I am pretty sure you could position your protestors within shot of the church,' I suggest.

'Yes, I will be sure to.' She nods.

I log on and notice that Marilyn's online petition already has almost two thousand signatures asking the council to reconsider their planning decision. I decide to give the followers an update on events and invite them to the protest tomorrow if they are free. The more publicity this campaign has, the better.

Not long after having done so, though, I worry that thousands of people will converge on the village tomorrow. Surely not? But if they did, it would be wonderful for the protest, I tell myself, wondering if the locals will appreciate a demonstration, and I fleetingly hope that an angry mob won't descend on the market square.

I get myself comfortable on my bed, and before long, I can feel my eyes become heavy with the effects of the gin. Afternoon drinking has never really been my thing, and before I know it I have drifted off into a deep sleep.

TWENTY-SEVEN

I wake up with a jolt to the sound of my phone ringing. When I focus my eyes on the caller display, I can see that it's Nathan.

'Nathan, hi.' I speak drowsily into the phone.

'You sound sleepy. Did I wake you?' he asks.

'I was just having a snooze – although it's probably wise I didn't sleep any longer, or I won't get any tonight.'

'How's the headache?'

'Um, oh much better thanks,' I reply, although in all honesty, after having two very generous measures of gin of the afternoon, I really do feel a bit sluggish now.

'Glad to hear it. I was just wondering if you have any plans for this evening?'

'Not really...'

'Then would you like to go to dinner? I would kind of like to continue our conversation,' he says eagerly. 'I am sure we have a ton of stuff to talk about.'

'I guess so, and I suppose I do have to eat!'

'Try and control your enthusiasm,' he jokes.

'Sorry, I never meant it that way. And yes, of course I would like to talk to you. How about Roberto's?' I suggest.

'As charming as Roberto's is, I know a place a short drive from the village. Shall I pick you up at seven?'

A glance at the clock shows four thirty.

'Why not. See you later then.'

I make myself a coffee, and wonder why Nathan wants to head out to another village. Could it be because he shows up at Roberto's with a different woman every weekend? At least that is if Will Sutton is to be believed. As I sip my coffee, I almost call Nathan back and tell him I can't make it after all.

I will meet Nathan later to be courteous and maybe tell him all about my life back in London. Tomorrow, I will be around for the protest and then make my way back to my apartment. This unplanned vacation has gone on for long enough.

I open an email that is inviting me to a party tomorrow evening in Shoreditch. Last-minute invitations often pop up, but usually when someone can't make it, and last-minute replacement invites are sent out.

I politely decline the invite, realising I am only a week away from Christmas Eve, when I am to review a new restaurant near the Shard.

Suddenly, I miss the glorious views from my apartment, especially at this time of year with magical decorations as far as the eye can see.

Whilst I have some time to spare, I give Mum a call, but it goes straight to voicemail. I am sitting thinking about her, when Sienna texts me from the studio.

Hey, how's it going? Are you home now?

Not yet. Resting here for a bit. Are u free for a chat?

Yep x

I call Sienna and after asking how the gingerbread competition went, she fills me in on the office gossip, and how an after an impromptu party after work on Monday, two colleagues got together and sloped off to a hotel.

'Both single, though, so why not?' She laughs. 'I'm a bit jealous to be honest; I hate being alone at Christmas.'

'Do you?'

'Yeah, not sure why, it just feels a bad sad...' she admits.

Last year, she was with a guy, but quickly dispensed of him in the new year, when she realised he could not get along with her son, which was, of course, a deal breaker.

'Fancy being my plus-one at a restaurant on Christmas Eve?' I ask her. 'I'm reviewing a new restaurant that has entertainment – see what it has to offer. You never know, there might be some fit single blokes. Then again, I don't suppose you want to leave your son on Christmas Eve.'

'It couldn't be more perfect! We're staying with my parents on Christmas Eve. They won't mind if I slip out for a few hours when Liam is in bed.'

'It's a date, then.'

'Ooh can't wait. And hope your ankle heals soon,' she says. 'Even though I can't imagine you will quite be up to dancing on Christmas Eve.'

'I shouldn't think so. Speak soon, then, bye, Sienna.'

'Thanks, talk soon.'

I freshen up and put on the long dress I bought this morning. I spray some perfume on ready to head downstairs to meet Nathan in reception, when there is a tap on the door.

I open it to find Nathan standing there, and he lets out a low whistle.

'Wow, you look amazing!' he tells me, taking in my long green patterned dress that is slightly low cut.

'Thank you,' I say. 'And you scrub up quite well yourself!'

The truth is, he took my breath away when I opened the door and saw him standing there. Even just wearing smart jeans and a shirt, with a blazer thrown over, he looks heart-stoppingly handsome. No wonder he has women falling at his feet.

TWENTY-EIGHT

'So where are we going, then?' I ask Nathan as, like a gentleman, he opens the door on the passenger side of his car and helps me inside.

'A Spanish place called The Cocina. I hope that's okay.'

'Perfectly, although I thought you might have preferred to stay local, so you could enjoy a glass of wine...' I comment as we drive. The thought that he doesn't want to openly be seen with me in the village also flits across my mind.

We drive past Roberto's, its large window strung with white lights and edged in red tinsel, making it look festive and inviting.

'I will have a small glass with my meal, but I don't mind; I am more interested in the food. And the company, of course.' He turns and smiles and it feels as though we have never been apart.

'So, I take it the wine tasting with the lady in your shop never took place?' I ask, deciding to take the bull by the horns and find out a little more about the attractive employee.

'It was no biggy; I can do that anytime.' He shrugs.

'Oh right, I won't lie, the disappointed look on her face made me think she was more than just an employee...' I tell him.

'It's complicated.' Nathan lets out a sigh, as we take a left turn out the village, passing the huge Christmas tree with the multicoloured lights, and follow a sign to another village.

'In what way?' I ask, suddenly thinking that I don't want to be in the middle of some complicated relationship thing.

'Jo is a brilliant employee; she is a wine merchant and has a real nose for good wines. I would hate to lose her.'

'And why would you?' I ask. 'Lose her, I mean.'

'She might decide to move on, when she realises there is no future for us.' He shrugs.

'Why would she think there was?' I ask. 'Sorry, I know it seems like twenty questions, but I would rather know if you were involved with someone else.'

'I thought we were just having a catch-up?' He smiles that dazzling smile.

'Well, yes, of course we are, but even so...' I say, before staring out of the window.

'Of course I am not involved with someone else,' he says, looking at me. 'I would hardly be taking you out to dinner if I was, would I?'

'Even as a friend?'

'Well, maybe yes, but I have no desire to settle down again with anyone at the moment,' he tells me honestly.

I decide to wait until we are inside the restaurant before I continue the conversation.

Driving down a country lane, we pass rows of houses with bushes and trees in their front gardens wrapped in lights. Windows with undrawn curtains are displaying Christmas trees, reminding me that Christmas Day is almost upon us. A half-melted snowman in a front garden is clinging on with the cold temperatures, and I wonder whether there will be any more snow.

I spot a tiny portable library the size of a large bird box, and my thoughts flit to the library in Brindleford. I truly hope it can be saved.

'So where are you spending Christmas Day?' Nathan asks as we approach the village.

'I'm not entirely sure,' I reply. 'I had imagined I would be spending it alone, as I am recently single.'

A car heading towards us is almost driving in the middle of the road, and Nathan presses his car horn loudly.

'There are some bloody idiots out there these days,' he says, shaking his head. 'Sorry, you were saying?'

'It doesn't matter,' I reply. 'You were asking me about Christmas. I have a couple of options, but I'm not quite sure how I will be spending the day yet.'

Soon enough, we have parked up in the restaurant car park and are heading towards the restaurant, its window illuminated with a yellow neon sign.

Once inside, I am met with a modern-looking restaurant with blonde wooden floors, and furniture in shades of blue and yellow. Soft lighting sets off the possibly too bright interior, although it all feels very stylish, and not something I would expect to see around here. Once more I am reminded how the village eateries are moving with the times.

We are shown to a cosy booth, and a drinks order is taken, after a menu has been handed to us and a bowl of olives placed down.

'Did you say something about recently being out of a relationship?' Nathan asks. 'Sorry, I had my eye on that idiot on the road.'

'I wasn't sure you heard.' I pop a salty olive into my mouth. 'And yes, we broke up about six weeks ago.'

'Not that long ago, then. Were you together long?' he asks.

'A few years, but in all honesty, I don't think things had been okay for a while. We were moving in different directions.'

'I know how that feels,' he says, with a raise of an eyebrow.

'We were just kids back then,' I remind him, even though I loved him with all my heart.

Our waiter reappears with drinks, before taking our food order. We've gone for a selection of tapas, and it turns out the same dishes caught our eyes.

'But it was real. At least it was for me,' says Nathan as he takes a sip of red wine. 'Don't you ever wonder how things might have turned out if you had stayed here?' he asks, searching my eyes.

It's a question I have asked myself over the years, but only when things haven't been going well in my life.

'It was for me too,' I reply softly.

Suddenly, there is the sound of singing and a waiter carries a birthday cake complete with sparkler to a nearby table.

We join in the singing, as a young woman with two gold balloons showing the numbers two and one opens her mouth in surprise and her table bursts into applause.

We say little as our first bowls of tapas arrive, and we both take in the words we have just spoken. How could a love so true be broken because I moved away, I wonder? Surely true love would have endured.

'Oh, to be that age again.' Nathan speaks first, as more bowls of tapas arrive. Terracotta pots containing fragrant paella sit alongside dishes of tomato and mozzarella salad, and sardines. The smell of a fragrant creamy chicken casserole has my mouth watering in anticipation.

'Would you really want to be that age again?' I ask, as I dip some bread into some olive oil.

'Twenty-one wasn't such a bad age for me,' he says, chewing some olive bread. 'I think it was the year I finally got over my first love and met Leanne.' He looks at me with a half-smile.

It occurs to me how much harder it must have been for Nathan living in the village, everyone offering their kind words to him over the end of his engagement, whilst I was able to slip away to the anonymity of the city.

'I wasn't with anyone for years,' I tell him truthfully. 'As I wanted to concentrate on building my career.'

'Which you did, most successfully,' he says kindly.

'I did. I was lucky.'

'A lucky break is one thing, but it takes hard work and talent to deliver,' he adds, reminding me of Henry's comment.

We stop talking to eat, and I can barely control myself from devouring the food greedily, as it is all so delicious.

'Well, I must commend you on your choice of restaurant; this food is amazing.' I spoon some more paella onto my plate.

'I'm glad you like it. I think at this time of year, it's nice to have a change of cuisine. I've eaten so much duck and turkey already,' he says as he forks some paella onto his plate. 'Not to mention Christmas pudding. It's my weakness, I'm afraid.'

'I remember.' I grin.

'You do?' He fixes me with his eyes as he takes a sip of Rioja.

'Of course. My mother was always pleased when you came around – apart from my father, you were the only one who ate her Christmas pudding.'

I recall her fussing over him and joking that she wished she had a strapping son like him to feed up. I never had a large appetite back then, and thinking about it, my father often preferred liquid lunches, apart from when she prepared a Sunday roast complete with his favourite Yorkshire puddings.

'But at least I will have him as a son-in-law,' she had told me when we became engaged. I think it broke her heart when we broke up.

I often wonder whether she might have stayed in the village, had Nathan and I married. Maybe even had children so that she could be the doting grandmother. The choices we make in life have so many consequences, but ultimately, I guess we all do what we believe will make us happy.

Nathan asks me about my life in London, and I describe my apartment and its stunning view.

'I'd love to see it, it sounds amazing!'

'It's a long way from here.' The thought of Nathan in my apartment has my pulse racing that bit faster. 'And don't you have a farm to run?'

'With good staff,' he tells me. 'It took a while to get the right people, but we have a great team now. It means I can take a short break if I want to.'

'And your father?'

'Oh he's still as strong as an ox. I think he is a long way from being looked after physically. It's the company on the farm he enjoys.'

We talk more about each other's lives and my career back in London, the place I now call home.

'I watched you on TV recently,' he reveals as we chat. 'In a baking programme. I even thought of having a go at the cranberry and orange cookies,' he reveals. 'I might still do.'

'So you really are something of a baker, then?' I ask in surprise.

'I enjoy it, yes. The boys used to go mad for my cakes and cookies, when they were little,' he says proudly, making me realise how little I know about his life now. 'In fact, they still do, when they come home.'

We talk easily for over two hours, grateful that there is no rush for our table.

'I can't believe you are really here,' Nathan says as he sips a bottle of alcohol-free beer. 'I wasn't sure you would show up, when I heard you had been invited to judge the gingerbread contest.'

I take in his handsome face in the candlelight and can hardly believe I am sitting here having a lovely evening. Nathan is so good-looking, it's hardly surprising he attracts a lot of female attention.

'I wasn't sure I would come...' I tell him truthfully.

'What made you hesitate?' he asks.

'I guess Mum no longer being here was a big factor. And I never really kept in touch with any of my old friends,' I explain.

I don't tell him the real reason for my hesitation in coming here, as I feel my cheeks redden.

'Well, I am pleased you changed your mind.' Nathan reaches across the table and takes my hand in his, and I feel a jolt of something in the pit of my stomach. 'Really pleased.'

He gestures for the bill then, just as a blonde-haired woman passes our table and says 'hi' to Nathan. She places her hand on his shoulder in a very familiar fashion, as she speaks to him.

Perhaps Will was right in saying that Nathan is playing the field since his divorce. It's probably a good thing I won't be around much longer to witness it, despite my undeniable attraction towards him. And didn't he say, just moments ago, that he is not interested in settling down with anyone? Maybe it's best to leave the ghosts of the past firmly buried.

After Nathan settles the bill, we are outside on the freezing cold street once more.

The shops here are like those in Brindleford, their windows decorated with lights and tinsel and reminding me that Christmas is just around the corner. I should have been home by now, but it seems that fate is intent on keeping me here.

A gift shop, its windows covered in snow-sprayed bells and snowmen, catches my eye as we pass. It occurs to me that there are no shutters on the windows of many of the shops around here, something I would never see in London.

'What are you admiring?' Nathan asks, looking over my shoulder. He smells so good, and I can feel the hairs on the back of my neck stand up from his closeness.

'That adorable little bear sitting on the log,' I say, pointing to the cute sculpture.

The gifts in the window are all carved from wood, and

include jewellery boxes, hand-crafted animals and wind chimes.

'I wouldn't like to meet one in real life, but this one does look cute,' agrees Nathan.

Soon enough, we are back at the car, and Nathan helps me once more into the passenger seat.

'I'm not sure I could stomach another alcohol-free beer,' says Nathan before we drive away. 'I have some good coffee back at the farm, though, if you fancy one?'

'Wouldn't we disturb your father?' I ask doubtfully. Didn't Nathan say his father lived with him at his cottage?

'He has his own quarters. More of an annexe in the grounds, but he likes it that way.'

'Coffee might be nice,' I reply, all the time wondering if I am doing the right thing.

'Perfect!' he says as he fires up the engine and we move off.

A radio station is playing songs of the nineties, and then a Christmas tune comes on that takes me right back to the school disco, and my first slow dance with Nathan.

'Remember this?' He glances at me with a smile on his face.

'Of course I do.' If I close my eyes, I am right back in the moment.

'You know, Stuart Simm was going to get you up for that slow dance, but I warned him off.' He grins.

'You did? You've never told me that before.'

Stuart Simm was the best-looking boy in the year back then, and all the girls fancied him, including me. That was before I fell head over heels for Nathan.

'He wouldn't have treated you right...' says Nathan with a shake of his head.

'You're probably right.' I smile, as after leaving school, Stuart quickly gained the reputation for being a bit of a heart-breaker.

You would have treated me right if I had stayed here, though,

Nathan Woods. I am certain about that, I think to myself, with a quiet moment of regret.

We speak little as we drive, lost in our own thoughts. The open curtains on the windows of several cottages have now been drawn, as people have retired to bed, making the road darker as we drive, so Nathan carefully negotiates the bends.

As we get closer to the farm, I suddenly feel a little nervous at the thought of being alone with him. Maybe I ought to ask him to drop me at the hotel...

However much I tell myself I am doing the wrong thing, we are soon swinging into the car park of Nathan's home. I am beginning to realise that as we become more reacquainted, I enjoy being around him. Maybe just one coffee, then I will head off.

TWENTY-NINE

'Wow, this is seriously nice!' I say as Nathan puts the key in the door, and we step inside the lounge from the front porch.

The cottage is set to the left of the driveway, adjacent to a field and next door to the holiday let.

'Thanks.' He smiles. 'I did have a little help with the interior design, but I did most of it myself.' He takes my coat along with his own and hangs them on black, cast-iron coat hooks in the porch.

I don't ask who helped him, but whoever it was has very good taste.

The cottage is a perfect mixture of traditional and modern, with wooden beams and a log burner, modern fashionable furniture and some beautiful lighting and mirrors that give the room a warm and comfortable feel.

After removing my coat and settling myself on a comfy cream sofa, Nathan heads to the kitchen.

'Actually, I have a bottle of really good brandy,' he says, popping his head around the kitchen door. 'Instead of a coffee if you fancy it?'

'Maybe a small one,' I say, as I already feel relaxed by the two large glasses of Rioja I drank at the restaurant.

'Coming up.'

I take a sip and feel the burn of the delicious brandy as the silky liquid slips down my throat. I can hardly believe I am sitting here in Nathan's stylish home. I carefully position myself on the sofa and Nathan tells me to flick a switch at the side of it.

'Recliner,' he tells me. 'And don't worry, it's a slow release.'

'Thank goodness, I wouldn't fancy being catapulted across the room, especially not with this leg,' I say, and he roars with laughter.

'Ah thank you, this is comfortable.' I give my approval as my feet are elevated, and I nestle into a cushion. Nathan throws a log into the burner, and soon enough the room is warm and toasty.

'Anything for you,' he says as he sips his drink. He is sitting on a chair opposite me, and we chat about this and that, including our parents. Whenever he tries to bring the subject around to what I want from the future, though, I find myself talking of something else, including the planned protest for tomorrow.

'I heard about that,' he says as he swirls his brandy around in his glass. 'I agree it's a shame about the library and the park. The boys used both of them when they were little. Although there is no doubt, the village needs more housing.'

'Maybe so, but surely there is a more suitable site. Anyway, there is a chance the decision might be reversed,' I add optimistically. 'If there is enough opposition.'

'It would seem very strange without a library in the village...' Nathan says. 'I hope the protest has some effect.'

'Me too. Or the village might end up with just one of those library boxes we passed earlier.' I sigh, suddenly realising how much I am invested in the preservation of the library.

I stifle a yawn as the warmth of the room seems to wrap me in a comfortable hug.

'Maybe I should get that coffee after all,' Nathan says, getting to his feet.

I nod as I feel my eyes become heavy, and I snuggle into the soft cushion. It's just so cosy here. Maybe I will just rest my eyes until Nathan returns from the kitchen...

THIRTY

I wake with a dry mouth, as a shaft of daylight pours through a gap in the curtains.

There is a heavy chenille throw over my body, and a glass of water on a table beside me. Good heavens, what time is it? Surely, I haven't slept on this sofa all night?

I carefully manoeuvre myself into a sitting position, hardly able to believe that I have spent the night here.

'Good morning, sleepyhead.'

Nathan appears with a breezy smile, carrying a tray of coffee, orange juice and some blueberry muffins.

'The muffins are made with my own fair hands!' he announces proudly and places the tray down beside me on the table.

'What time is it?' I ask, as I get my bearings. I must have been really exhausted to fall asleep like that. Perhaps I should never have mixed wine with the brandy.

'Just after eight.'

'Eight o'clock? I can't believe it,' I say as he pours me a coffee from a cafetière. 'Why didn't you wake me last night?' I ask.

'You just looked so comfortable.' His eyes crease upwards into a smile. He is dressed in lounge pants and a T-shirt, his hair lightly rumpled. 'Well, as comfortable as you could be.' He glances at my ankle.

For a second, I imagine how I would have felt waking up in the same bed as him this morning, wrapped in his arms, before I push the picture out of my mind. I have seen for myself how easy he is around women, and the admiring glances he attracts. Do I really want to get reacquainted with someone like that when I am hundreds of miles away from home?

He helps me up and I head to the loo on my trusty crutches, my evening bag tucked under my arm. At least there is a downstairs bathroom, I tell myself thankfully, as I wash my hands and stare at my reflection on the mirror. Gosh I look rough. Last night's make-up has all but disappeared from my face and I have panda eyes. I freshen up as best I can, before returning to the lounge.

'I have a big day today; I really ought to be off.' I'm thinking of the protest later outside the library. 'I imagine you need to get on too.' I take a bite of the delicious muffin.

'I do. The shop only opens at nine thirty, and it is a slightly later start in the winter months. The workers will be arriving soon to pick some more parsnips, though – we sell a ton of them at Christmas as you can imagine. I'll drive you back. I'll grab a quick shower while you finish your coffee, if that's okay, though?'

'Sure,' I say, realising I will be back at the hotel around nine, where I will have the small matter of encountering June at reception. The walk of shame in last night's dress, even though there was nothing shameful about the whole evening... It would hardly be the most romantic encounter anyway, with my ankle in this stupid cast.

Damn it, why did I have to fall asleep here? Although I'm not sure why I am worrying about looks from June. I'm sure she doesn't give two hoots about my private life. And why should I worry if she does? I guess it is just a reminder of how easily you can become the subject of gossip in a small village.

I polish off the delicious muffin, amazed that Nathan really made it, before I finish my coffee. I've learned that Nathan is a good businessman, a master baker, and as good looking as he ever was. What else there is to know about him? He seems almost too good to be true – and I suddenly find myself wondering what led to his divorce.

There is thankfully no one behind the desk in reception, so I slope to my room and flop down onto my bed, my head spinning.

I go over last night's events in my mind, recalling our date in the restaurant, and how wonderful it all felt. I remember Nathan taking my hand in his, and the pulsating effect it had on me. I am sure we would have kissed back at the cottage. If I had not fallen asleep, that is – but then what?

I imagine him covering me in a blanket as he returned from the kitchen, and I cringe. I bet his other dates don't do that. I have an image of him entertaining other women at the cottage and find it one I don't care for.

Managing to take a shower and carefully dressing, I am styling my long hair in the mirror when Marilyn calls. Thankfully, one of the things I take with me everywhere is my hair-taming gel, which allows me to style it into smooth curls.

'Morning, Ruby, how are we this morning?' she asks chirpily.

'Marilyn, hi, I'm good thanks, and you?'

'Yes, fine thanks. So, are you all set for later? I have just had a call from the regional news station, who have informed me they will be here at noon to set up and do a sound check. Oh, and everyone has been busy making banners for the protest, especially the children; they look rather wonderful.'

'That's fantastic. Let's hope it all has some effect.'

Marilyn had approached the council inviting a representative to attend the meeting, but they have, as predicted, declined.

'I do hope so,' says Marilyn. 'I suppose all we can do is try. It would be awful to give up without a fight.'

I sit thinking about the protest later, when I receive a text from Nathan:

Have you thought any more about staying on at the cottage? X

His message makes my stomach roll, and at once throws my mind into turmoil. Do I really want to be staying so close to Nathan? Would I be able to resist him if we spent time together in the evening?

It takes me a while to reply, and when I do, I simply tell him that I will speak to him later about it.

Just after eleven, I feel the need to call Mum. I hope she isn't in the middle of the fields or something. On the third ring she answers.

'Ruby, hi, darling, is everything okay?' she asks.

'Yes, fine, Mum. Are you free to talk?'

'As it happens, your timing couldn't be better. We have just finished some cleaning up and are about to take a coffee break.'

I'm not exactly sure how Mum will help, but after spending time with Nathan, I just feel the need to speak to her. She adored him so much when we were younger. That was all such a long time ago, though.

'So how are things there?' I ask her.

'Pretty much as they were the other day when you called

me. The elephant calf is still doing well. So, I suspect that is not the only reason for your call?' she says knowingly.

'Well, maybe not entirely... The thing is, I bumped into Nathan yesterday.'

'Ah, the one you were always so careful to avoid. How is he?'

'He's good. Doing very well in fact.'

'Is he married?' she asks, as I hear water being poured in the background.

'Are you sure you aren't busy?' I ask her.

'I've told you, it's break time. I'm just filling a kettle,' she says, before I hear her talking to someone else. 'There, someone else is going to make the coffee now, so I am all yours. Only instant coffee for now, as our coffee machine is broken, but never mind. So, were where we?'

'You asked if Nathan was married. He is divorced,' I explain.

I realise it is something I would never have known, had I not returned here.

'I see. Does he know you are currently single? Did you chat long enough for him to know that?' she presses.

'We did. In fact, he took me to dinner last night.' Once more, I go over the gorgeous evening in my head. 'The food, the lighting and ambience in the restaurant, it was all just perfect,' I tell her.

'Ah I see, so you really had a good catch-up then,' she says. 'And how did it feel spending time with him, after so long?'

I wish I could tell her that it was pleasant enough to catch up with an old friend, but nothing more.

'Oh, Mum, it was lovely. All that time I tried to avoid him, but I guess things were raw back then.' I sigh. 'There has been a lot of water under the bridge since then.'

'But did you still feel something when you were with him?' she asks. 'Because you do know that true love never dies.'

'I guess I did feel something, yes, although I wish I didn't...' I long for her to be here in person instead of at the other end of a phone.

'Why do you wish that?'

'Because it felt good being near him. Wonderful in fact. But my life is in London. I guess I just don't want to get hurt all over again.'

'You clearly don't believe in fate, then?' I can imagine her smiling at the other end of the phone.

'Not usually, although I have wondered why I have ended up coming back here. And I guess it has taken my mind off my broken ankle.'

I realise then that I hadn't told Mum about that as I didn't want to worry her, being so far away.

'You've broken your ankle?' she asks in surprise.

'Yes, I slipped in the snow.'

'Oh Ruby, why on Earth did you not tell me? Are you alright?'

'Yeah fine, it's just a real inconvenience. I guess I didn't want to worry you...'

'I'm your mother,' she says softly. 'I love you and I care about your welfare, no matter how many miles there are between us. I hope you know that.'

I can feel a lump form in my throat. I know Mum loves me even though she rarely says so. It feels good to hear it out loud.

'Of course, thanks, Mum,' I say quietly. 'And sorry if it's selfish of me, but I kind of wish you were here in Brindleford with me. Marilyn was asking about you too,' I tell her.

I wonder whether I ought to have left the subject of her returning here out of the conversation, as well as speaking of Marilyn, as Mum is quiet for a minute.

'I have been curious over the years,' she admits. 'Although maybe a little like you, I did not want to revisit the ghosts of my past.'

'I get that,' I say.

'I wasn't sure you would fully understand,' she tells me then. 'But you are old enough to know that not all of my memories in Brindleford are good, especially with your father. But Marilyn was a good friend. She got me through some dark times, as did Gerard, before they were a couple. I should get in touch with her, if you think that she would like that.'

I wipe away a silent tear that has slid down my cheek. 'I know she would.'

'In the meantime, do what makes *you* happy, Ruby,' she advises. 'You know how much I loved Nathan, as did you. If you feel any of that love again, I think you should follow your heart. Life is far too short to do anything else.'

THIRTY-ONE

'Amanda, hi!' I say to Amanda Lewis, who gives me a hug, and I take in her floral, expensive perfume.

It's bitterly cold and she is wearing a brown faux fur coat and heavy make-up, looking more a model than a TV presenter. The rest of the crew are muffled up with heavy coats, scarves and beanie hats as they set up their cameras.

In front of the library, quite a crowd have gathered, including children brandishing brightly coloured home-made banners bearing the words *Save our library*. I do hope the publicity today will make the council realise how important it is to the village and revoke the planning permission on the new housing.

There is not quite the influx of people I imagined would appear, after the social media reminder, but there is still time, I guess.

Marilyn is chatting to a cameraman asking him if there is any possibility of getting in a shot of the church, as I join her. He tells her he will do if someone is chatting to Amanda about the library, and she immediately asks me if I will do the honours.

'I mean, you grew up with that library,' she reasons, when I remind her that I am hardly in a position to protest, as I don't live here anymore. 'What would you have done without those first books?' she asks me. 'You might never have gone to university, had you not discovered books.'

'Maybe you have a point,' I say, recalling the librarian ordering in books for my course at college.

'And imagine what it might do for the cause, a famous person joining the fight to save a library. It would not do your reputation any harm either, would it?' She eyes me.

'There is nothing wrong with my reputation, thank you,' I say, mock horrified.

'You know what I mean. People would have a newfound respect for you, I'm sure, supporting the plight of a local village in danger of losing their library,' she says, using all her powers of persuasion.

'I'll have a think about it...' Really, there is no reason why I should not say a few words. It's not as if I am endorsing anything dubious after all.

Before we know it, Amanda Lewis has given the backstory of the library and its possible demise, speaking confidently into the camera. She has come a long way since she covered for me during my illness.

Marilyn, who has been nominated as a spokesperson, appears then, ready to say a few words. As she speaks, a steady swarm of people begin to descend upon the village, carrying banners and chanting 'No more government cuts.'

'Gosh, where have all these people come from?' Gerard asks, as they pour along the street towards the library. Their chanting is becoming so loud, I worry they will drown out the sound of Marilyn on camera. Once more I fear I may have invited a mob with extremist viewpoints.

'Maybe it's not a bad thing...' I try and reassure myself, although I worry that if their protest becomes troublesome, there is barely a policeman in sight. I can only hope things remain civilised.

Marilyn beckons me over, as a cameraman follows her to a spot where the church is in full view in the background, just as Gerard duly walks into the camera shot.

'So why is it important to you that Brindleford village library is saved?' asks Amanda Lewis as she thrusts a microphone under my face.

'I think it's important every child has access to books from a young age,' I say. 'As a child, I was a frequent visitor to the library myself.'

The noise from the background protestors is gaining momentum and Amanda is struggling to hear, and places one hand over her ear as she speaks.

'No more government cuts, no more government cuts!'

'Having a library in the village as I grew up inspired my love of reading. Not to mention having access to books and a place to study as a college student,' I say. 'And it isn't just for borrowing books; a whole host of activities take place there, especially in the school holidays,' I add as the noise from the protestors grows louder.

'I bet there is no such problem in London,' Marilyn chimes in. 'I bet the British Library is not under threat. It isn't fair that up North money for the arts is usually at the bottom of the pile,' she says firmly.

'Talking of bottom!' Gerard exclaims, his mouth gaping open.

We follow his gaze to a guy who is running in front of the crowd, as naked as the day he was born. As he draws closer to us, he raises his banner, before mooning in front of the camera.

Flashbulbs are going wild, as one of the few police officers in attendance manages to remove the unexpected streaker from the scene. Marilyn has her hand over her mouth, but her shoulders are shaking with laughter; children are openly squealing with mirth, whilst their parents try and cover their eyes. All I can think of is that the guy must be absolutely freezing to death.

As the news reel comes to an end, out of the corner of my eye, I spot Nathan across the road near the post office, taking in the whole scene. And standing next to him with a look of amusement on his face is Will Sutton.

'You were great, a true professional,' I say to Amanda, as the news item wraps up; and the protestors from outside the village seem to have disappeared as quickly as they appeared.

'Do you think so?' she asks doubtfully.

'I do. You carried on like a real trooper, even when the flasher ran past.'

We both burst out laughing.

'That was something I was most certainly not expecting.' She shakes her head. 'Especially in this weather. And it's live too, so will have gone out to everyone in the Yorkshire region.' She grimaces.

'Honestly, I think it will not go unnoticed how well you handled the situation. Next stop, the national news.'

'Well, I can but dream.' She smiles.

I chat to Amanda for a few more minutes, wishing her well, before she heads off with the rest of the crew.

'I think they got a good shot of the church. It's a shame Gerard never got the opportunity to talk about the next service, though.' Marilyn grins.

'Maybe better to stay on topic,' I gently remind her once more. 'Although you at least got the church in shot and it looks marvellous with the Christmas tree and the nativity scene outside.'

'I suppose so.' She smiles. 'Do you think the news item will have any effect on the council decision on the library?'

'I'm not sure, but at least they will know how the people of the village really feel.' I wonder if it will make any difference, but we have to try.

'Anyway, let's get home and watch it; I've recorded it. Are you coming?' she asks.

'Could you give me ten minutes?' I say as I spot Nathan walking towards me.

'Of course.' Marilyn touches my hand. 'And I will understand if you become otherwise engaged,' she says, winking as she spots Nathan.

THIRTY-TWO

'Well, that was quite the story.' Nathan grins.

'I guess the villagers have done all they can!' I shrug. 'They have a petition too, which is gaining some serious attention online.'

'Do you fancy a coffee?' He gestures to the bookshop café.

'Sure, it might warm me up a bit,' I say, walking beside him slowly on my crutches.

Inside is as warm and comforting as I remember, and I can smell a hint of cinnamon. At the counter I see there are gingerbread lattes for sale, so I plump for one.

Seated in a corner, away from the window, we enjoy our warm drinks.

I glance at the gingerbread latte, which is almost a dessert, topped with whipped cream, marshmallows, and a mini gingerbread man poking out of the top.

'I saw you chatting to Will Sutton earlier...' I say, as I attempt to drink my latte without wearing a cream moustache. 'I didn't realise you knew him.'

'I don't know him exactly. But I know who he is,' he tells

me. 'As most people around here do. We were chatting about the demonstration mainly.'

'And what did he say?' I ask, keen to know how he felt about it all.

'Not a lot. He did say he was surprised by the reaction, though, as he reckons he has personally spoken to lots of people around here who are desperate for housing,' Nathan reveals.

'Well, he would say that.'

'Actually, I don't disagree with him... Although I do think he might have chosen somewhere other than the library and park.'

'Exactly.' I nod in agreement.

'Perhaps land around here is hard to come by,' he suggests, 'and the council would sell land in a heartbeat to a developer, especially if the library is under-used and costing too much.'

'It's not always about money.' I sigh.

'But sometimes it is. The council are only given so much money, that they must spend wisely.'

'That may be, but it will be sad to see it go. It hosts all kinds of activities in the summer holidays.'

'Well, it isn't over yet,' he reminds me. 'And maybe they could find another venue for that sort of thing.'

'Will spoke about you too,' Nathan says as he takes a sip of his coffee.

'He did? What did he say?'

'He said you made your feelings clear that you were against the plans, when you went for a walk together.' He raises his eyebrow.

'Oh right, yes.' I can feel my cheeks burning.

'So how do you know him?' he asks.

'He didn't tell you?'

'Why would he? As I said, he just dropped in the fact that you mentioned the planning, whilst out walking together.'

'I drove his father here from London. Or more accurately,

we shared the driving.' I tell him all about the train problems and how we ended up travelling here together.

'I sort of got the impression he likes you.'

'I don't think so.' I shake my head.

'Well maybe he thinks I am a decent person, accompanying his dad here from London, but I'm sure that's all.'

'He seemed very interested when you were talking to the reporter. He could barely take his eyes off you.' He grins.

'Are you sure it wasn't the reporter he was looking at? She was very attractive.'

'No, it was definitely you,' he insists.

'Perhaps he was interested in what I had to say. This housing development is a big deal to him, remember.'

'If you say so.' He smiles. 'Anyway, I can understand why he might like you. He would be mad not to.' He holds my gaze, and I feel suddenly feel flustered. 'And he was keen to let me know that you went for a walk together.'

'And did that bother you?' I find myself asking.

'Perhaps it did. Anyway, I kind of told him you weren't looking for romance.'

'Why would you say that?' I ask, surprised.

'Because, Ruby Holmes, it's obvious he fancies you, and I hate the thought of you dating someone around here, if it isn't me,' he says candidly. He reaches across the small table and takes my hand in his. 'And that, I am afraid, is the truth.'

'Nathan. Please don't.' I draw my hand away from him, despite the tingles I feel all over.

I can't fall for him all over again, I simply can't. And there is the small matter of me hearing he is always out with different women. At least that's what Will has led me to believe – unless he had an ulterior motive.

'I'm sorry if it isn't what you want to hear, but there it is... I never expected to feel the way I did when I saw you again after so long,' he tells me. 'Are you telling me you don't feel something too?'

'I'm not sure what I feel. It's complicated,' I say.

'It doesn't have to be,' he replies softly.

'But my life is not here anymore; I just don't see how things could possibly work.' Though a part of me wishes I could take the risk and just stay here forever.

I bring the subject back to the library, my thoughts all over the place, but Nathan is keen to talk some more about us.

'Things might not work out the way you want them to, but I guess that's life,' he says as he finishes his coffee. 'We don't always get what we want, do we? I know that more than anyone.'

He glances at his watch then and tells me he must leave. 'How long will you be staying in Brindleford?' he asks, searching my eyes.

I want to tell him I will stay on at the cottage at the farm. I want to tell him I would love to spend more time with him, and see how things go, but I don't. Instead, I tell him I will be leaving tomorrow morning for London.

'Then maybe I can see you this evening?' he asks.

'I'm not sure that's a good idea...' I tell him and he takes his jacket from the back of his chair and leaves.

THIRTY-THREE

'But why would you be dashing back here? I thought you were getting along?' Coleen says down the phone line.

As soon as I got back to the Swan Inn, I messaged Coleen and asked if she is free, and she called me at once.

'We are. That's the problem.'

'How is that a problem?' she asks, confused.

'Oh I don't know.' I sigh. 'I don't see how things could work with my life being in London, and he definitely has no shortage of admirers. Besides I kind of wanted to be on my own for a while, after Ade, and not rush into something else,' I explain. 'That's always a disaster.'

'But love often turns up when we least expect it. And it isn't as if you don't already know Nathan, is it?' she reasons.

'But we have both changed.' And yet he still stirs something inside of me.

'Don't we all over time, but deep down I think we are basically the same. Besides, didn't you tell me one evening that you and Ade had been limping along for a while?'

'I suppose that is true. Ade was craving his old lifestyle,

there was no doubting that. I still think I ought to remain single for a bit, though. Gosh, why did I even come here?'

I could have enjoyed my own company back home, taken time out and avoided the angst and uncertainty that a new relationship can bring. Especially when the other person lives hundreds of miles away. But maybe running or pushing people away to focus on my career isn't what I want to do anymore – maybe there's a middle ground.

'Oh Ruby, maybe you ought to give things a chance and just see what happens. Life's too short...'

'My mum said the same thing. But I have worked so hard for everything I have; I can't just give it all up.' I sigh.

'Who said anything about giving things up?' she asks. 'You could write your column from anywhere, and don't you only film for a day or two for *Britain's Best Cook*? Surely you could commute or stay over here on the odd days you have restaurant reviews. No one is suggesting you give up your apartment. Besides, isn't there a break in filming until the next series?' I realise that what she is saying makes sense.

'Yes, filming for the next doesn't start until the spring.'

'So surely you have time to work out how you really feel? A couple of restaurant reviews up now and then is doable surely?'

'You make it sound so simple.'

'It could be!'

'Are you trying to get rid of me?' I joke.

'As if. I have missed you already,' she says kindly. 'But you must do what is right for you.'

After finishing my call, I pack my things into a case. And book my train ticket online. Maybe back in London away from Nathan, it will give me a chance to work out how I really feel.

I call Marilyn and tell her I will be getting the connecting train to Leeds, to catch the two o'clock train for London.

'I'll be keeping my eye on things, but you will let me know how the decision goes with the planning, won't you?' I ask.

'Of course I will, as soon as I find out. I am going to miss you, Ruby. It's been so lovely getting reacquainted.'

'I think so too. And I promise to come back in the spring, when those daffodils appear,' I tell her, raising my eyes heavenward, asking to be forgiven for telling a white lie, as I really can't see myself coming back here anytime soon. If ever.

Sienna calls as I am getting ready, telling me she will have to pass on the Christmas Eve night at the restaurant as she has a date.

'Sorry, I hope you don't mind... A new sound technician started at the studio a few days ago, and we seem to have hit it off,' she says excitedly. 'He has invited me to a Christmas Eve party.'

'Of course I don't mind, I'm happy for you. Besides, it's a work thing for me really. You might have got bored after a while.'

'I'm sure I wouldn't have. Anyway. I'm glad you don't mind. So, are you heading home soon?' she asks.

'This afternoon. I think I need my own bed now.'

'I can imagine. You were only meant to be there overnight, weren't you?'

'I was.'

I can hardly believe I have been here less than a week as so much has happened in that short space of time.

'Well, you can tell me all about it when you get back to London. Maybe we could meet somewhere for a drink, as you won't be back in the studio for a while,' she suggests.

'Sure, I'd like that. And you can tell me all about your budding romance.'

'Let's see how the Christmas Eve party goes. If he doesn't like dancing, it might be already doomed.' She laughs.

After speaking to Sienna, I trundle my case into reception and say my goodbyes to June.

'Ah it's been lovely having you here, love; I hope you will come and stay soon,' she says, wrapping me in a hug. 'It's been exciting having a celebrity in the village.'

'Maybe I will, and thanks for everything, June, I really appreciate it.'

I take a call from my agent then, who lets me know that the restaurant review for Christmas Eve has been cancelled, due to a fire at the venue.

'Extensive damage apparently,' she informs me. She tells me that the word on the street was that the fire had been an insurance job, as the restaurant had been limping along for months. It seems the Christmas Eve party, complete with first-class entertainment, had failed to attract the ticket sales they had hoped for.

I head down to reception to meet Will – after I texted Henry to inform him that I was finally leaving, Will kindly offered to bring my case to London when he drives his dad home in early January. I'm grateful he did, as I would have really struggled with my crutches – something I hadn't thought about.

'So you are finally leaving, then...' says Will as he greets me in reception.

'I am. And thanks for this. Are you sure you don't mind dropping this off at my apartment?'

'I don't mind in the slightest,' he assures me. 'It will give me a chance to see you again,' he adds with a cheeky grin. Maybe Nathan was right about him being interested in me after all.

'And you must bring Henry too!' I suggest, deciding it's best if we aren't alone. 'I can return the favour by making you some lunch.'

'Sounds good. Bye, then, Ruby, safe journey home,' he says. 'Actually, can I drop you at the station?'

'It's a two-minute walk,' I say, 'but thanks.'

As he disappears, I think to myself that Will might have been someone I could have been interested in, despite the library situation. That is, if I wasn't, annoyingly, so hung up on someone else.

THIRTY-FOUR

I arrive at the train station a little early, and take in the platform, with its old-fashioned waiting room that reminds me of the station in the movie *Brief Encounter*. In the summer months, raised beds that line the platform are filled with colourful flowers, earning it the honour of the UK's best kept station for several years running.

The café is open, but I decide to stay outside sitting on the bench, as I feel like breathing in every last minute of the Yorkshire fresh air before I head back to London.

I glance at the board that tells me the train will be arriving in eight minutes, so I take my phone out and scroll through it to pass the time.

I would never have thought I would still be here – my original plan was to be in and out of Brindleford. A part of me curses the weather, although another part of me is pleased to have made friends with Marilyn again. And there is no denying the attraction I felt for Nathan, who seems to be taking up most of my thoughts.

With a minute before the train arrives, I heave myself up onto my crutches, when I hear someone shouting my name.

Glancing at a footbridge, I can hardly believe my eyes when I spot Nathan. He is suddenly running down the stairs and arrives on the platform just as the train pulls into the station.

'Ruby, wait,' he pleads. 'Don't leave yet.'

'Nathan, my train is here; I must leave,' I say, as several passengers step off the train. I know I literally have a minute or two until the train departs.

'I don't want you walking out of my life for a second time...' he says, a pleading look on his face. 'And in the same place too. Please say you will stay for a little longer.'

'But, Nathan, I must go.' As the passengers disembark the train, the seconds are counting down.

'I'll drive you to London, tomorrow if you like. Or the day after, whenever you like.'

'I really don't think I can, I...'

I am silenced then, as Nathan's lips finally meet mine, and the sound of the guard's whistle seems to mingle with the sound of the fireworks that are currently pinging around my body. I am almost transfixed to the spot, locked in a moment that I do not want to end, before the sound of clapping brings me back to reality.

I turn to find several people cheering, and I feel like I am in the scene of a romantic movie.

'You were saying...?' he asks when we finally come up for air.

'I think I might have missed my train,' I reply, my heart beating like crazy.

When the people from the train drift off, Nathan kisses me once more, and we stand there all alone on the platform, wrapped in each other's arms as my train vanishes into the distance. And despite my uncertainty, being here right now just feels right. Maybe London can wait a little longer.

. . .

'So where is your luggage?' asks Nathan as we walk to his car, my head still spinning.

I tell him all about Will offering to deliver it when he drives Henry back to London.

'Any excuse to see you again, I'd say. I told you he liked you.'

'He was being practical.' I roll my eyes. 'I couldn't have managed my case on these crutches, and as his dad's place is only ten minutes from me, he told me it was no problem at all.'

It occurs to me that I will need my case back, if I am to stay here a little longer.

'If you say so.'

Once seated in his car, Nathan leans in and kisses me once more, and I feel the familiar heat throughout my body. Despite all the reservations, I am happy that Nathan turned up at the train station, and I have to ask myself: why am I so intent on running away? Apart from my work, what exactly would I be running home for? Suddenly spending Christmas alone with that cheeseboard doesn't seem quite so appealing.

I expect Nathan to take the two-minute drive to the farm, but instead he turns off onto the main road that leads away from the village.

'Where are we going?' I ask in surprise.

'Just taking a detour, to get your luggage back. As you will be staying on, I guess you will need your clothes – unless you are planning on walking around naked,' he jokes.

'Very funny.' I roll my eyes. 'I was actually just thinking about that. Do you know where Will lives?'

'Everyone knows where he lives. It's not exactly your run-of-the-mill terrace, as you already know.'

'I suppose so, but does he know we are coming?' I ask a little doubtfully.

'Does he need to?' He turns to me. 'As you are simply collecting your suitcase.'

'No, maybe not.'

'And I am saving him the trouble of driving across London to deliver it to you personally,' he adds.

'You're not jealous, are you?' I ask him.

'No. Should I be?' He turns to look at me.

'Not sure,' I say as I flick my hair over my shoulders. 'I am footloose and fancy-free after all.'

'Hopefully not for long,' he says, studying my face. 'Unless you really want to be?'

'Not sure...' I tease.

When we eventually swing into the driveway of Will's house, he is just heading out through the front door.

'Ruby!' he says in surprise as I wind down the window of the car. 'What are you doing here?'

'Nathan just drove me over for my luggage. It seems I am staying here a little longer.'

'That's great news,' he says, as Nathan steps out of the car.

I open my car door to chat to him as Henry emerges through a side gate.

'Hello, Ruby, love, I thought I heard your voice,' he says as he approaches. 'I was in the garden feeding the birds.'

'Hi, Henry, how are you?' I ask, delighted to see him.

'Fine, fine. Just filling the bird feeder before I settle down to a couple of old episodes of *Columbo*. You can't beat it on a cold afternoon in front of the fire.' He smiles. 'So, what you doing here then?'

'It seems Ruby is staying on a bit longer,' Will updates him.

'Ah so will you be going to the Victorian market tomorrow?'

'Gosh yes, I had forgotten about that... Tomorrow you say? Then yes, maybe I will.'

Will returns with my case, and I thank him.

'Not a problem.' He smiles. 'Oh and if you are still here for New Year's Eve, you are most welcome to come to my party. Both of you that is,' he adds, turning to Nathan.

'Thank you,' I say.

'So you think you might still be here on New Year's Eve?' Nathan asks as we swing out of the driveway.

'I could be...' I shrug. 'But I guess I do have to go home sometime. So, do you fancy Will's party, then?'

'Possibly. Although maybe it is more exciting to be in London for New Year's Eve?'

'I do enjoy it,' I confess. 'I usually head down to watch the fireworks at the Embankment, but this year with my broken ankle, I might just view them from my apartment with a glass of bubbly.'

'Alone?' he asks.

'I could party with friends, but actually, yes, I think alone this year, which I actually don't mind... These past few days here have been a little exhausting.'

'You don't have to be alone,' he says. 'I would be happy to pop open the champagne.'

'You would come to London?'

'Why not? I have always meant to visit London. And what better time than for New Year?'

'You've never been to London?' I ask, surprised.

'Strangely enough, no. I have visited lots of places in Europe, and Florida with the boys when they were younger, but London seems to have eluded me.'

'It's a wonderful city. I would love to show you around. When my ankle is better, that is. But I thought your boys were coming to visit?'

'They are, but only for Christmas week. They are heading back to their respective universities in time for a big New Year's Eve party apparently.'

I suddenly feel nervous at the thought of meeting his sons, should he decide to introduce us as anything more than friends.

'So what do you think? You have sold me the idea of drinking champagne and watching the fireworks from your apartment...' His eyes dance, and I can picture the romantic scene unfold in my head.

I think of my mother and Coleen, telling me how fate steps in. Now that the restaurant review is cancelled, it seems the stars are aligning.

As we pull into the vast farm, I glance around and realise once more what a success Nathan has made of his life. Who knew that we were both as ambitious as each other.

I glance at the huge green barn, currently lying empty, and wonder what Nathan will do with it eventually. Perhaps he could extend the shop even more. They could sell some of his cakes, given his baking skills.

After carrying my case inside, Nathan pours us both a brandy, and I gratefully sip it beside the fire. I am just making myself comfortable, when there is a tap on the front door.

Nathan lets an older man inside, who I can see at once is his father.

'Hello, Ruby, it's been a long time,' says Ben Woods as he shakes my hand. He still has a full head of hair, now snow white, and a handsome face. He looks like an older version of Nathan.

'It really has. How are you?' I ask.

'Can't complain. Life's been good.' He nods. 'Apart from when Nathan's mother passed, then things were a bit bleak. But we must get on, don't we?' He physically stands up straight and pulls his shoulders back. 'And this one here has looked after me well.' He pats Nathan on the shoulders and smiles. 'So will you be joining us for Christmas lunch?' he asks.

'Hopefully, yes,' I find myself saying, and a smile spreads across Nathan's face.

'I was hoping you would say that,' he replies.

'Good to see you, Ruby.' Ben takes my hand and shakes it once more before he departs.

Nathan and I sit talking for hours, and after taking a shower,

I wish I had some lounge pants to relax in. I mention this to Nathan, and he offers me a pair of his, and a long T-shirt that I gladly change into.

'Very sexy,' he teases when I emerge from the bedroom wearing his black joggers and the too-big white T-shirt.

'It will have to do. But perhaps I need to go shopping again tomorrow.'

'I'll drive you to a bigger town tomorrow if you like...' he offers.

'Do you know, I think I will shop local.' I want to support the shop on the high street again. 'The shop in the village was actually pretty good,' I say. 'And I would love to go to the Victorian market.'

'I was actually going to suggest that,' he says. 'I usually have a stall there, selling Christmas plants and wreaths.'

'But not this year?'

'No. The farm shop has really taken off, so I don't see the need. Especially as the stall spaces are limited. I thought I would leave room for other traders,' he explains.

'That's very benevolent of you.' I smile.

'Well, it is Christmas. Some local crafters only manage to sell their wares through local markets.'

Nathan is thoughtful too. Another quality to add to the list of his charms.

'So, do you still see Brindleford as the backwater you left behind, then?' he asks me.

'I never thought that exactly... But I must admit, I am impressed with what I have seen so far,' I tell him, realising the place has a vibrancy to it that I never expected.

We talk until night falls, when Nathan pulls me into his arms on the sofa and kisses me deeply.

'I have just realised, I never showed you the bedroom last time,' Nathan whispers in my ear, before he stands and takes me by the hand and assists me to the bedroom. 'I hope it is to your liking.'

'I am sure it will be,' I say, feeling that familiar excitement in the pit of my stomach.

As he pushes open the door, I take in the stylishly decorated room, once more a mix of traditional and modern. The bed at the centre of the room is huge.

'So,' says Nathan, standing behind me, his arms wrapped around my waist as he kisses my neck. 'Will it do?'

'It will, it's beautiful.' I gently remove his arms from my waist and turn to face him.

'But maybe we both ought to get some rest; I imagine you have an early start,' I say, and he silences me once more with another thrilling kiss.

'I'm glad you stayed, Ruby,' he breathes.

'Me too, but I don't want to us to rush things,' I tell him, half-heartedly, as my stomach rolls over in anticipation.

'No, of course not.' He grins.

'Because I won't be here forever, you do know that,' I remind him.

'Yes, you said,' he mumbles, as he kisses my neck, and it feels so good.

'Just so we are clear,' I say, my head swimming.

'Ever heard of taking one day at a time?' he asks as he locks eyes with me.

'Yes, but...'

'Yes, but what?' He is looking at me in such a way, I can barely string a sentence together.

'I really can't remember.'

'Thank goodness for that,' he breathes, as he closes the bedroom door, and leads me to the huge bed.

THIRTY-FIVE

I slip into a deep sleep, wrapped in Nathan's arms, before waking in the early hours of the morning.

I manage to quietly swing my leg over the bed, and slip on Nathan's long T-shirt, before I use the bathroom and quietly head to the kitchen.

It's a little after seven in the morning, and from the kitchen window, I take in the glorious sunrise appearing above the fields. A barn is silhouetted in the early morning sun, as a flock of birds fly overhead. It's all so calming and peaceful.

Just then, a robin jumps onto the window ledge outside the kitchen window and startles me. I suddenly recall the blackbird flying through the window the first time Nathan showed me the cottage. Little did I know then that I would be spending the night here.

I flick the kettle on, before rummaging in a cupboard. I find some muesli, so carefully open the kitchen window, and the cheeky robin stays put as I place some seeds onto the windowsill.

I think of all the people who believe the appearance of a

robin means someone you love is near, and briefly think about my dad.

'You will never get rid of him now,' Nathan says as he appears in the kitchen, rubbing his eyes sleepily.

'Why would I want to? He is just adorable.' I watch the robin enjoying the unexpected treat.

'Just like you.' He pulls me to him and kisses the top of my head. 'You okay?' he asks.

'Just fine,' I say, sinking into his embrace. 'You?'

'Couldn't be better.' He smiles just as the kettle flicks off. 'I'll make the tea,' he says. 'We can take it back to bed if you like.'

After taking a shower, I receive a text from Marilyn, telling me how much she enjoyed seeing me again, and hoping I had a pleasant journey. I give her a quick call.

'Actually, Marilyn, I never quite made it home. Again.'

'Oh my goodness, is everything alright? You haven't fallen again?' she asks with concern.

'Not exactly.'

I wonder why I feel like a teenager who is about to tell their mother she has a boyfriend.

'I am staying at the accommodation on Nathan's farm. I would have called you later.'

'I see,' she says, and I picture her grinning knowingly. 'So will you be here for Christmas?'

'I might be,' I tell her. 'And it means I will certainly be here tomorrow for the council announcement.'

'Well, I think it's wonderful. You and Nathan, I mean,' she says kindly. 'I always thought you two were made for each other.'

'Thank you, Marilyn. Will I see you later at the market?'

'You will indeed. The church choir will be singing, and I

will be handing out the church newsletter with details of our Christmas services.'

'Never one to miss an opportunity, hey,' I say, and she giggles.

'Absolutely. See you later, then. I am thrilled you are staying on.'

THIRTY-SIX

The marketplace is already crowded when we arrive. Nathan's arm is threaded through mine, as I make my way carefully along the cobbled street.

'Gosh, this is just as I remember it!' I say, taking in the rows of stalls facing each other along the square, the traders all dressed in Victorian costume.

The smell of chestnuts roasting nearby drifts towards my nostrils, as I stop and admire some handmade wooden toys on a stall. Spinning tops and wooden puppets painted in bright colours sit beside each other and a jewellery box with its lid open is playing a merry Christmas tune.

The stallholder with a handlebar moustache, and wearing a waistcoat and pocket watch, wishes us a good afternoon and doffs his top hat as we stop and peruse the things on his stall. He tells me he supplies the toy shop on the high street with some of his wooden toys.

'I've admired those!' I tell him. 'They really are beautiful.'

'Thank you. And I can take commissions, for that perfect gift,' he says, handing me his business card.

I'm delighted to find Penny from the bakery at a stall selling gingerbread men, slices of Christmas cake and some Christmas cookies.

'Ruby, hi!' She beams when she has finished serving a customer. 'I see you are still here, then.'

'It seems I can't manage to get home,' I say. She says 'hi' to Nathan, who she knows, and we chat for a couple of minutes, before I buy three slices of Christmas cake, and some white chocolate cookies.

'Who is the third slice of cake for?' asks Nathan.

'Your dad. Unless you are now going to tell me that you have baked a Christmas cake?'

'No, they are a little time consuming... I might knock up some mince pies, though.' He grins.

The sky above is dark grey. The day might be described as gloomy, were it not for several Victorian-style streetlamps along the street, and lit candles on stalls.

We stroll past stalls selling all manner of things that include food, hand-knitted gifts, and home-made Christmas tree baubles. Lotions and potions give off a delightful aroma as we pass a stall, and I treat myself to a jasmine-scented soap, served to me by a lady wearing a long black dress and a Victorian bonnet.

The smell of pulled pork at a stall has my stomach rumbling, so Nathan buys us a filled roll along with some mulled wine.

A crowd is beginning to gather near the clock tower, ready to listen to the choir who have just arrived. We manage to find a bench to sit on, courtesy of a young couple who notice my injury, and offer me their seat and I thank them.

I take in the choir members as we finish our rolls and sip the delicious mulled wine. The gentlemen are wearing long heavy coats and top hats, the women dressed mainly in full red skirts, shawls and velvet-lined bonnets.

'I feel as if I have stepped back in time.' I sigh, as the melodious voices of the choir fills the square, giving me a warm cosy glow inside.

Nathan curls his hand around mine and right at this moment, there is nowhere I would rather be.

When the choir finishes to thunderous applause, we move around the market stalls once more. A fit guy walks past carrying a Christmas tree, and I can't help but laugh.

'Are you checking out the guy with the Christmas tree?' asks Nathan, following my gaze.

'No, it just reminds me of a scene in a Christmas movie,' I explain. 'There is always a guy carrying a tree, usually for some hapless woman'

'Do you watch a lot of those movies?' he asks as we walk.

'Sometimes, although usually when I am ill,' I tell him. 'The TV ones can be really bad.'

'I could find a good one on Netflix if you want to watch one later,' he offers. 'I will even let you choose.'

'You would watch a Christmas romcom with me?'

'I would sit watching paint dry, as long as you were next to me.'

'Oh please.' I roll my eyes. 'That sounds like a line from one of those really bad films.'

'Sorry, was that too much?' He laughs.

'Just a bit.'

The greyness of the day is suddenly replaced with a gentle glow, and when I look upwards, I spot tiny fragments of snow in the light of a Victorian lamp.

'Look!' I say to Nathan excitedly, pointing to the sky.

Within minutes, thick white snowflakes are swirling to the ground as people gasp in delight. Soon enough, it will look like a scene from a Christmas card.

I whip my phone from my bag and take some photos of the magical scene that I want to remember forever. London suddenly feels so far away.

I spot Will and Henry in the crowd, and wave as they make their way over.

'I bet you're pleased you didn't miss this,' says Will, glancing around at the heart-warming scene.

'Indeed I am. Victorian markets seem much more authentic up here. Maybe it's because of the snow.'

I glance around at some children who are scooping up snow in their hands and playfully throwing snowballs at each other.

'Maybe we had better make a move soon, though,' suggests Henry. 'That snow is showing no signs of stopping.'

'You're probably right,' Will replies. 'Maybe see you at my New Year's Eve party.' He smiles.

'I'm not sure what my plans are yet, but thanks again,' I say warmly.

Before we leave, I head to the clothes shop on the high street, just as the owner is locking the front door.

'Oh you're closed!' I say, disappointed. 'I guess I should have come earlier.'

'Hi again!' says the shop owner. 'I've been at the market, so I closed early today. I just nipped back for my hat, as it started snowing,' she explains. 'I can open for ten minutes if there is something you particularly need?'

'If you're sure, then thank you. I am just after some loungewear.' I remember spotting a nice selection the last time I visited.

She ushers me inside, and less than ten minutes later, I'm armed with two lounge suits and a pair of cosy socks, and we are outside on the pavement.

'Thank you so much!' I tell her.

'No, thank you,' she says. 'I never expected any more sales today. Merry Christmas.'

'Merry Christmas to you too.'

.   .   .

Later back at the farm, Nathan invites his father for coffee that we enjoy with the Christmas cake. He had decided to stay home today as his knee was playing up, but insisted we went out.

'That's very good,' he says appreciatively as he takes a slice of cake. 'You can't beat a good Christmas cake.'

I think back to Mum making her cake when I was young, and how Dad would sip the brandy as she did so. I also think of our phone call, when she shared how bittersweet her memories are, even though I know that she loved Dad dearly. I certainly remember lots of laughter in my childhood when I was growing up, so perhaps his problems only worsened in later life.

'Anyway. It's a good job I stayed around, as some visitors arrived a little earlier than planned. Ten minutes ago in fact.'

Right on cue, there is a tap on the door, and in walk two young men.

'Dylan, Joe, what are you doing here?' He stands and crushes his sons in an embrace.

There is no mistaking the fact they are twins, or that they take after their father. Their likeness to him almost takes my breath away, as I am catapulted back in time. It seems the male gene in the Woods family is particularly strong.

'We decided to get an earlier train,' explains Dylan. 'Thought we would surprise you.'

'Well, you have certainly done that.' Nathan smiles, clearly thrilled to see his sons. 'Oh and, boys, this is Ruby; she is renting the cottage over Christmas,' he tells them.

Renting the cottage. He makes it sound so businesslike.

'Hi.' They both smile broadly. 'Hope you enjoy your stay,' says Dylan, who I get the impression is the more outgoing of the two.

'Thanks,' I say, glancing at Nathan, who doesn't really make eye contact.

'So what are your dinner plans?' asks Joe. 'I'm starved.'

'Nothing new there, then.' Nathan smiles. 'We can have a

takeaway if you like, as you are rather earlier than expected. What do you fancy?'

'Chinese?' suggests Dylan and the others agree.

'Would you mind taking the boys to the cottage?' Nathan asks his dad. 'I'll be over in a minute.'

'Sure,' Ben replies as he stands. 'And thank you for the cake.'

Nathan turns to me and says, 'You don't mind, do you?' after they leave. 'You could join us for the takeaway if you like, but I haven't mentioned you to them yet. I will do, though,' he assures me.

'No, of course, don't worry.' I paint on a smile. 'I'm shattered anyway – an early night is probably on the cards for me,' I reply, thinking of how I will be watching that Christmas movie alone.

'I'll speak to you soon.' He gives me a quick kiss, then heads off.

As I sit alone, I let his words sink in. He hasn't mentioned me to the boys, and he has just introduced me as someone who is simply renting the cottage over Christmas. Is that all I am: a lodger who comes with benefits?

I give myself a talking-to then, realising I am just being silly, and that he is probably telling the boys about me as we speak. At least I hope so.

THIRTY-SEVEN

Just over an hour later, as I am settling down to watch a film, there is a tap on the cottage door.

'Do you still like sweet and sour chicken?' asks Nathan as he stands before me. 'I included it in the banquet that has just arrived. You must come and join us,' he offers.

'I'm not sure...' I tell him. 'It's your first evening with your sons; I'm sure you have a lot to catch up on.'

He deserves some alone time with his sons. I feel guilty for thinking earlier that Nathan saw me as someone who simply is renting the cottage.

'We have spent the last hour doing just that. Well, at least I have told them who you really are, which is quite up there as news goes,' he tells me as he steps inside.

'You have? What did they say?'

'They think it's cool that you were my first girlfriend. And Dylan said you are really pretty, and that I am punching above my weight, the cheek.' He laughs. 'So, are you joining us? The food will be getting cold.'

'I guess so,' I say, wishing I had maybe refreshed my make-up, but thought I was spending the evening alone.

'I feel a bit nervous,' I confess as I grab my coat to join him for the short walk to his place.

A bit nervous is actually an understatement. I feel sick at the thought of getting to know his sons. I don't have a lot of experience talking to young men.

'There is no need to be anxious. The boys want me to be happy. They have seen their mum settled, and I know they would like that for me too,' he assures me. 'In fact, I have never introduced them to anyone else.'

'Really?'

'Nope. Sure, I have been out on a few dates, but I have never met anyone I was interested in enough to introduce them to the boys. Until now,' he reveals.

He circles his arms around my waist and pulls me in for a kiss.

'Okay,' I say, my head spinning, as it does every time he kisses me. 'Let's do it. It's ages since I have eaten sweet and sour chicken.'

THIRTY-EIGHT

As the conversation flows, and the boys tell us stories of their time at university, any nerves I may have felt have completely disappeared.

Both boys seem to be enjoying their respective courses and have made some good friends.

'So, what are your future plans?' I ask, thinking that some young people remain in the city where they studied.

Dylan is the first to answer. 'Not sure,' he says, as he sips a beer. 'I might get some management experience with one of the big supermarket chains if I can, as they pay well. Then when you are old and doddery,' he teases, turning to Nathan, 'I can manage this place.'

'You don't have to wait until then, you know,' Nathan replies. 'Maybe I could take early retirement.' He grins.

'At the age of forty?' His dad laughs. 'You would be bored stiff after five minutes.'

'Well. Okay. Maybe ease off a bit. Perhaps I could take up golf.'

'I can't quite see that,' says Joe. 'Didn't we all try it once, and you put a ball through the clubhouse window?'

'True enough.' Nathan chuckles. 'Maybe not golf, then.'

Joe tells me he would like to work with farm animals in his role as a vet, as he enjoyed being around the cows when he was growing up at Hope Farm.

As the night draws to a close, I suppress a yawn. When Nathan's dad stands and announces he is off to bed, I decide to take my leave.

'I'll walk you back,' says Nathan.

'Well, it has been an absolute pleasure meeting you both,' I tell the boys as I stand. 'See you soon hopefully.'

'Yeah, it's been good to meet you too,' replies Dylan and Joe agrees.

'I won't come in, at least not this evening. Even though I would love to be climbing into that bed with you right now,' Nathan says, as he nuzzles my neck while we stand on the doorstep of the cottage.

'I understand.'

'Although I might sneak out in the middle of the night, like a naughty teenager.'

'Maybe best not to do that. Not unless you want to frighten me half to death.' I poke him playfully.

'Okay.' He circles his arms around my waist and pulls me to him. 'I guess I will just have to settle for a kiss.'

He kisses me beneath the light of the silvery moon, and I know more than ever that I belong here with him.

For now, at least.

The next morning, I barely see Nathan as he is busy in the farm shop ensuring everything is ticking over nicely in the run-up to Christmas.

I had taken him up on his offer of calling in this morning if I got bored, and when I arrive, the lady who had been inviting him to sample some wine is refilling a fridge and Nathan is standing next to her chatting. I notice her throw her head back and laugh at something he has just said, as I approach them.

'Ruby, hi,' he greets me with a kiss on the lips, and the lady shoots me daggers, as she places some cheese into the large fridge.

'I thought you would be resting up?' he asks.

'I am tired of sitting around, and you mentioned I could call in.'

'Of course. I am just a little busy, but come on, let me show you some new stock that has just arrived,' he says, leading me away.

He didn't look so busy standing around chatting, I think to myself.

We head to a section of the shop that has a good selection of gifts, from teddies and soft toys wearing Christmas hats, to luxury food hampers and jars of sweets lined up on shelves. There are boxes of shortbreads and candied jellies that remind me of Christmases from days gone by.

'You would be surprised how many people come in here for a last-minute Christmas gift. Which is why I always order a delivery of gifts about now. Although not too much just in case it doesn't sell.'

'Ever thought about a Boxing Day sale?' I ask. 'There are those people don't see relatives on Christmas Day itself, but over the festive season, who might like to bag themselves a bargain,' I suggest.

'That's a brilliant idea,' Nathan replies. 'I normally only discount items in the new year, but you're right, word would soon get around if we opened on Boxing Day, for the morning at least. There is probably a lot of fresh produce that could be discounted too,' he adds, the more he thinks about it.

'Exactly. A morning sale, then you can spend the rest of the day doing whatever you like. We are a nation of shoppers after all.' I think of the Boxing Day sales in London – although maybe things are a little different around here.

'We all normally take a long walk on Boxing Day,' he tells me. 'Which I would love you to join us on. We kind of pick at cold cuts and cheeses in the afternoon, with a glass or two of wine.'

'It sounds perfect, but I am sure I would hold you up...' I say, once more cursing the day I fell onto the ice.

'I would walk at your pace,' he offers kindly. 'If the others want to go on ahead, that's fine.'

'Well, let's see, shall we?' Although I wonder what else I'd be doing.

'Or we can stay at home. We could have that privacy then,' he suggests, with a raise of an eyebrow.

He puts his arms around my waist and kisses me gently on the lips, and I can feel some of his employees glancing over.

It is the day before Christmas Eve, and people are out in force buying their fresh vegetables and table decorations for the big day, and I notice a woman placing a food hamper wrapped in cellophane into her trolley. Nathan is right about those last-minute shoppers.

'Do you fancy a bit of a games night later?' he suggests as we escape to the café for a quick coffee.

'At the pub?' I ask.

'No, at my place. A bit of Trivial Pursuit, then we generally take a vote on a second game. I'm hoping Exploding Kittens will get the vote.' He grins.

'That sounds horrible.' I gasp.

'Don't worry, it's simply a card game. No kittens are actually blown up.' He smiles.

'I would like that, but are you sure you don't want to spend time with your boys alone? They aren't here for that long after all,' I tell him sincerely.

'I would love to have you there,' he insists.

'I know you would.' I reach across the table and take his hand in mine. 'But honestly, I really don't mind. Spend time with your boys. I might give Mum a call and have a catch-up with her.'

'If you're sure,' he says. 'Now that you are staying here for Christmas, I guess we will have lots of time together. And as I have introduced you to the boys, I can spend the night at the cottage if you like.'

'Sleeping with the tenant?' I laugh. 'Talking of which, you haven't actually told me how much I owe you for the rental,' I say, thinking he will be missing out on money from another possible tenant whilst I am there.

'Don't be silly. I guess I panicked when I first introduced you, as the boys coming home early took me by surprise. But now they have met you, I am pretty sure they will soon love you as much as I do. I wouldn't dream of charging you a penny for being here.'

I try not to read too much into his words. He hasn't actually told me that he loves me, and I am not sure what I would say if he did.

Realising how busy things are at the farm shop, I head back to the cottage, to sort through my clothes and do some washing. I am barely there five minutes, when I have an incoming call from Marilyn.

THIRTY-NINE

'Just letting you know that the council have told me there will be change to their decision. It seems only the person submitting the planning has the right to appeal, which I suspected was the case.' She sighs.

So the protest had no effect at all...

I picture Will Sutton celebrating his victory, although maybe he already knew we were fighting a losing battle.

'So will the closure be imminent?' I ask.

'The end of January,' she tells me. 'Which will at least give people the chance to get their heads around it. I am sure there will be a huge book sale too. If there is, I will encourage people to buy them. I can store some here until we find a suitable site to set up our own community library,' she says positively.

'But that's a wonderful idea! A community library.'

'More of a book recycle centre, to be more accurate. I have seen this work in other places. It is pretty much a book swap, which means we will not often provide brand new books, but it is better than nothing. And I guess we could fundraise to purchase new books.'

'Oh Marilyn, that all sounds wonderful,' I say, admiring her positivity.

'I think it could work. And if we can find big enough premises, perhaps the social groups could continue too,' she adds. 'It will take a lot of hard work, but doesn't everything that is worth doing?'

'Of course it does,' I agree. 'And I am pretty sure everyone in the village would get behind it,' I assure her.

'I think so too. As soon is Christmas is over, I shall be calling a meeting at the village hall. And then the search for a suitable venue will start. Maybe charging a small amount for the books could cover a modest rent somewhere. We can only hope, but I have faith that the good Lord will provide,' she says optimistically.

'I am sure that's true,' I say, just as an idea suddenly pops into my head.

I finish a few chores, then call Mum but the call goes straight to voicemail. She is probably busy working, or preparing for Christmas, and she did tell me that she would give me a call this evening, though. I wonder how they spend Christmas in Kenya, and if Mum will miss any of the English traditions.

I can hardly believe it is Christmas Eve tomorrow. Or that I am spending Christmas here in Brindleford with Nathan, the person I was so keen to avoid. The thought of sitting around the dinner table with Nathan and his family on Christmas Day fills me with a warm glow.

I had offered to help with lunch, but Nathan wouldn't hear of it. Apparently, his dad is also a good cook, so he told me that between them, they have it covered.

'So you can put your feet up,' he had told me, the morning after he had stayed over, and we were discussing Christmas plans.

I had offered to do the washing up, but he shook his head, telling me that he has a dishwasher that the boys would be loading on the day.

'So you see,' he had told me as we finished our drinks in bed that morning and he placed my cup down and took me in his arms, 'you can simply relax and enjoy the day.'

I bring myself back to the present by sitting on an armchair peering out of the lounge window. The ground is still covered in snow, and I spot a robin sitting on the fence. I wonder if it is the same one that appeared on the window ledge in the kitchen.

An hour later, after having a FaceTime call with Coleen and filling her on events here, I video call Mum once more, and she picks up.

'Hi, Ruby, I was going to call you when I'm free, sorry it's later than I planned – I've been on vegetable peeling duty.'

'No problem, I am glad to hear your voice. Is everything okay?'

'Oh yes, fine. All okay with you?' Mum asks.

'Yes thanks, although it looks like the library is to close in early January.'

'That is simply awful. I have so many happy memories taking you there as a child.' She smiles.

'Oh I know, me too. It's a shame but Marilyn is determined to find other premises and set up a community book cycle.'

'That sounds like Marilyn,' Mum says, smiling.

'She asks about you a lot,' I tell Mum, who says to say 'hi' to her next time I see her.

We chat for a while longer, with a promise to have a quick chat on Christmas Day.

Shortly afterwards, there is a knock at the door and Nathan is on the doorstep.

'If you are not coming for the games evening, at least let us have dinner together.' He brandishes a brown paper bag. 'I haven't eaten all day, it's been so busy. I'm starved.'

'That's a nice idea; what do you have?'

'Chicken, ham and leek pie,' he says, lifting it from the bag. 'Some greens, and mash too. Ready-made but from a luxury brand.'

A short while later, as we sit eating our food, I tell him all about the library decision.

'I'm sorry to hear that,' he says as he tucks into his food. 'Although I had a feeling that the protest wouldn't change things.'

'You did?' I say as I devour the delicious pie.

'I'm afraid so.' He nods. 'But it was nice to witness the solidarity of the villagers.'

'I agree. Marilyn is organising a meeting after Christmas. She is hoping to find a permanent home for a community library, although rental costs might mean that is out of the question.'

'Hmm, I can see that being an issue. But I am sure something will turn up.'

'I do hope so.'

When he finally leaves, I am suddenly overcome with tiredness. I was awake early this morning, and even the smallest tasks leave me tired dragging this cast along with me.

I get myself ready for bed and finally settle down to watch a Christmas movie.

I think about Nathan, and his comment about how all the villagers stand united when facing a problem. And it feels rather nice to be a small part of that.

FORTY

The following morning, Nathan is tapping on my door brandishing coffee. I am only just out of the shower, having slept until eight thirty.

'Morning, sleepyhead.' He laughs as he walks inside.

'How do you know what time I woke?' I ask, puzzled.

'I knocked earlier, although I guess six thirty was probably too early. I was on my way to one of the fields to collect more veg,' he explains. 'Those parsnips and sprouts were flying off the shelves yesterday.'

'I see. And thanks for the coffee, it's most welcome.'

'I missed you last night...' he tells me as he draws me in and kisses me.

'I missed you too, but I think I needed an early night.'

'You smell really good.' He hugs me close to him.

'That will be the jasmine soap from the Christmas market,' I tell him, as he unbuttons my blouse.

'Jasmine suits you,' he murmurs, leading me to the bedroom.

. . .

'I hate leaving you like this, but Christmas Eve is one of our busiest days,' Nathan says later as he gets dressed.

'Don't you worry. I am quite happy here for now, although I was thinking of going to church later.' I'm not a regular church-goer, but I have always loved a church service on Christmas Eve.

I am propped up on the luxury pillows, sipping my now cold coffee.

'Although I now feel a bit like a wanton woman.'

I suddenly think of Gerard all those years ago and his sermon about Jezebel.

'Shall we go to the eight p.m. service?' suggests Nathan. 'Midnight mass is no more, but I enjoy the evening service.'

'Are you sure? I would love that.' An evening service would be magical, with all the lights from the village streets and the Christmas tree outside.

'Of course,' he says, giving me a kiss before he departs. 'See you later.'

It is just after three, when I nip to the farm shop and return to the cottage with some fresh provisions that I put into the fridge.

I am sitting with a cup of tea, when it occurs to me that I could come up with some recipes, using produce from the shop. Maybe I could start a blog, and share the comings and goings of the farm, throughout the seasons. If there is enough interest, a local TV station could even feature the farm in regional news stories.

Later as we stand in the church for the evening service, I realise I have everything I want for Christmas, and it fills me with a warm glow. Well, almost everything. The demise of the library is sad news, but I've had an idea coming together about it since my call with Marilyn yesterday. I am pretty sure I could find the perfect place for a village library to relocate. I just need to speak to someone first.

FORTY-ONE

'I'm not particularly religious, but I think I would just like to say grace, if that's alright,' says Ben Woods as we sit down for our Christmas lunch.

He gives thanks for the food we are about to receive, and for bringing families together, as he glances around the table.

'I have to say, I never thought I would be sharing a table with you this year.' Ben grins at me as he prepares to carve the turkey. 'But sometimes in life, things can go full circle. Just like this waistcoat I am wearing that is back in fashion. You would pay a fortune for this in a vintage shop,' he declares, which has us all smiling.

We raise our filled glasses and wish each other a merry Christmas.

The table is beautifully decorated, with gold-coloured plates and expensive-looking gold and white crackers. A splash of colour is added in the form of a chunky red candle as a centrepiece, along with some red napkins.

The table is groaning with a veritable feast that includes turkey, ham, and an assortment of homegrown vegetables. Dishes of sprouts and parsnips, along with golden roast potatoes and pigs in blankets, are enough to make my mouth water. We pass our plates to Ben, who slices the meat and slides them onto our plates.

'Gosh, this looks fit for a king,' I comment as I eye a dish of tasty-looking cauliflower cheese.

I tell everyone about my mum being in Kenya for Christmas this year, and Joe says it is something he would love to do once he is qualified.

'Would you?' says Nathan, looking a little surprised.

'Why not?' Joe replies. 'I am pretty sure I want to work with farm animals, but it might be a good experience, to figure out what I really want.'

'I think it's definitely important to figure out what you really want in life,' Nathan advises his son.

I can feel him glancing over at me, before he refills our glasses and my face flushes.

As the meal draws on, talk turns to the village and the imminent closure of the library.

'I can't say I'm surprised if I'm honest. There has been a couple of clowns running that council for a while now,' Ben reveals. 'Totally mismanaged the budget by all accounts.' He tucks into some Christmas pudding. 'They barely have the money for the potholes in the road leading out of the village. And do not get me started on the trucks that drive down it. I'll be dead before they build the bypass they have been considering.'

'Oh dear,' whispers Dylan to Joe. 'We have set Grandad off now.' The boys start to clear the table ready to stack the dishwasher and kindly make us all some coffee.

'Anyway, regarding the library' – I turn to Nathan, as I sip some coffee – 'I have an idea I was thinking of running by you.'

'Oh, yes?' he says, an intrigued look on his face.

'Have you ever considered doing something with the old barn?'

'Once or twice. But I guess I am always so busy, I never really get around to actually doing something about it. Why?'

'I was just wondering if it could be used as a temporary library type building, for the villagers.'

'A library?'

'Well. More of a community hub really,' I explain. 'Marilyn mentioned looking for cheap-to-rent premises, and a kind of book cycle, selling cheap books, then returning them. It has worked in other places apparently... She thinks the library will sell off a lot of their books cheaply.'

I notice Nathan doesn't really answer my question as to what he might do with the barn. But if he is as invested as he says he is in the community, then maybe he will seriously give it some thought.

Later at the cottage, I have a FaceTime call with Mum and we wish each other a merry Christmas.

'Go and pour a drink. Let's have a toast!' Mum is wearing a red paper party hat.

I pour myself a Baileys and push it towards the screen, where she raises her glass of red wine.

'Have you had a nice day?' I ask her, and she tells me all about the food she has eaten with all the other volunteers.

'Not quite turkey with all the trimmings, but quite delicious all the same. So when will you be heading back to London?' she asks. 'Although I imagine it will be hard to tear yourself away from the village now,' she says knowingly.

'I think it will.' I sigh. 'Nathan would like to come to London on New Year's Eve and watch the fireworks. His sons will be returning to university for their own parties, though, which means he will be leaving his father alone.'

'He doesn't need to be alone. There is usually a bring your

own drink and food type event at the village hall on New Year's Eve. I am sure he knows everyone.'

'Probably...' I say, thinking I am almost tempted to spend New Year here myself.

After wrapping up the call, I head to bed reflecting on what a wonderful day it has been. And what an unexpected way to spend Christmas.

FORTY-TWO

Nathan calls me in the morning to ask if I am up for the Boxing Day walk.

'But first, I would like to show you something, if you're up and dressed,' he says, leaving me intrigued.

Fifteen minutes later, he has arrived at the cottage.

'So where are we going?' I ask, surprised that we are not heading to his cottage, or climbing into his car.

'Just around the corner,' he tells me, as we make our way towards the shop. Soon enough, we are standing outside the huge green barn.

'I have been thinking about what you said,' he explains as we stand looking at the empty building. 'About the community hub.'

'You have?' I say, my heart soaring.

'It kind of makes sense to use it for something for the village, as it is only sitting empty. So, shall we take a look?'

I wasn't sure what I was expecting when we stepped inside, but the huge barn is spotless. It is completely empty apart from a load of hay bales in one corner.

At once, I can imagine walls lined with bookshelves, and chairs dotted about.

One end of the barn lends itself to a counter selling drinks and cakes, in my mind's eye. It could be wonderful.

'So what do you think?' he asks. 'Obviously, the hay bales would have to go.'

'Would they?' I say, an idea suddenly springing to mind. 'Maybe you could leave them there for the children to play on? Especially in the wet weather, when they cannot use the playground outside...' I suggest. 'And over there, you could serve drinks and cakes.' I point to the end of the barn. 'Maybe even rustle up some of your own to sell.' I realise I am getting completely ahead of myself. 'I could even make a few myself, although I am a little out of practice.'

'You seem to have things all figured out,' says Nathan with a smile on his face. 'I think I am a bit too busy to supply the cakes but we already have a supplier that serves the café. And I am sure Penny would like an outlet for her cakes, if she has the time to make them.'

'Maybe she could do with an assistant...' I say idly.

'Are you offering?' he asks.

'What? No, of course not.' I laugh. 'Although you never know. So do you think it is doable, then?'

'I definitely do!' he says. 'And a counter selling drinks and snacks would generate some money.' He rubs his chin. 'Unfortunately I don't have the time to get involved in such a project, but if Marilyn and some of the other villagers wish to do so, then yes, let's make it happen!'

I practically leap on him, as I wrap my arms around him and pull him in for a kiss.

'You are the best! I can't wait to tell Marilyn. In fact, I will FaceTime her now!' I say excitedly.

· · ·

Marilyn lets out such a scream of delight at the news, it has Gerard rushing into the room to check that she is alright.

'Nathan Woods, you will surely get your reward in heaven,' she tells Nathan, who is smiling at her reaction.

'I haven't told you how much the hire of the barn is yet,' he says.

'Ah.' She frowns. 'But I am sure it will be reasonable.'

'I am joking.' He grins. 'It will be free of charge, but I am thinking visitors to the hub might buy a drink, or pop into the shop and spend some money, so maybe I am not as benevolent as you think.' He grins.

'Well, you have made my day, that's for sure. I can't wait to chat about it later. This is the best Christmas present ever.'

'You never fail to surprise me,' I tell Nathan as we enjoy our crisp winter walk.

There are still clumps of snow clinging to the grass, although the footpaths are clear.

True to his word, he walks at my pace, with Ben and the boys are up ahead of us. We follow the river around the village, greeting several other walkers as we do so.

'Is that a good thing?' he asks, as he curls his hand around mine.

'Up to now, it is, yes.'

'You haven't surprised *me* too much,' he says, suddenly stopping and facing me. 'Because I knew all those years ago how wonderful you were. And still are.'

Despite the chilly weather, I feel a warm glow inside.

Up ahead, we notice Dylan and Ben on a footbridge, dropping sticks into the river and watching them disappear beneath the bridge.

'Pooh sticks, that takes me back,' says Nathan as he watches them. 'Nice to see they haven't outgrown that...' He smiles.

'It seems there are some things we never really outgrow,' I tell him.

'I couldn't have put it better myself,' he replies, as he pulls me in for a kiss.

'Just look at that buffet.' Marilyn stands back and admires the variety of food on the tables of the village hall. 'It just shows what a community can do, when they all come together.'

It's New Year's Eve, and as news of the new community hub has spread, the village have decided to pull out all the stops and have the best New Year's party ever. We decided to put New Year in London on hold but there is always next year.

Even Will Sutton has donated several cases of champagne and paid for a firework display.

He had suggested to Marilyn when he ran into her in town that he might abandon his own party and come to the village hall instead.

'That might be nice, as people seem to have forgiven you, regarding the library,' she had told him.

'That's because it's a win-win situation,' he had reasoned. 'New houses, and a new reading room for the villagers '

'I suppose so. And the fireworks have probably gone some way to appeasing folk too,' she had said. 'They were too costly this year.'

We have the most marvellous evening, listening to the talented band that play an assortment of music styles and have everyone on their feet. Will has brought Henry along, who has danced the night away with various women.

'That was interesting,' Nathan tells me as he returns from a chat with Will Sutton and clutching a bottle of beer.

'Oh, yes?'

'He was asking if I have any land to sell,' he reveals as he sips his beer.

'And do you?'

'I do as it happens. A couple of acres beyond one of the crop fields.'

'I presume he wants it for housing?'

'That's right. Two luxury homes. Which would be in an idyllic location, I suppose. The views from the bedrooms would overlook the river...' he muses.

'Sounds wonderful. So what do you think?' I ask.

'I think I could agree to it, if he builds one luxury home. I can think of someone who would certainly enjoy living there,' he says, with a slow nod of his head.

'Oh right. Who?' I ask, as the penny slowly begins to drop.

'Me of course. My cottage is really only big enough for one.'

As the countdown to the New Year begins, I think of all that has happened in such a short space of time. I also think of my apartment in London, that suddenly feels cold and empty, despite its luxury interior and impressive location.

The words of Nathan's father, and how he spoke of things going full circle, pop into my mind and I have come to realise that what is meant to be will be, however we may try to fight it.

'Happy New Year!'

There are congratulations and hugs all around, as above our heads, rockets turn the dark sky into a sea of pink, green and cascading silver stars.

As I glance upwards, with Nathan's arms around me, I can almost hear Gerard and Marilyn telling me that God moves in mysterious ways. And I think to myself that maybe he does just that.

EPILOGUE

'So how does it feel being back in London?'

I am having lunch with Coleen in Soho, a few days before filming starts for *Britain's Best Cook*.

'Good actually. It feels energising in a different way to Yorkshire.'

'I can imagine. You are so goddam lucky as you have the best of both worlds,' she says, and she is right.

I decided to keep the apartment in London – my work is here after all – but I spend a lot of time in Brindleford now. And it so lovely having a second home in the city, as Nathan and I can escape here at the weekends. I also started the monthly blog, detailing the comings and goings of the farm, along with some delicious seasonal recipes, which is proving to be very popular with an ever-increasing following.

The building is going ahead for the luxury new home in the spring, so after that, I am hoping to make Brindleford my permanent home. But with regular visits to London, of course.

At Christmas, Nathan had presented me with a ring.

'It's an eternity ring,' he had been keen to explain. 'Just so you don't feel trapped.' And I had told him I was no longer that eighteen-year-old girl, and that there was no danger of that.

'So, you will be happy to live here at least some of the time?' he had asked, and I told him without hesitation that I would. I love him more than I would have ever thought possible.

The community hub has been a massive success too, and as Marilyn had predicted, the sale of the old library's books has filled many of the shelves, which some of the villagers had kindly erected.

A rota of willing volunteers has been drawn up to serve coffees and cakes, with locals such as Esme often donating their own bakes.

Mum came to Brindleford too once Christmas was over, and we exchanged gifts and had a Sunday roast at the Swan Inn. She has happily become reacquainted with Marilyn and some of her old friends. And the best news? She is considering moving back here permanently, since I have taken up with Nathan.

'I don't think I have ever seen you look so happy,' says Coleen as we finish our drinks.

We have enjoyed a lovely lunch and will be heading home before the evening crowds fill the streets. 'I am thrilled that you return to London often, though; I would miss you if you didn't.'

'I would miss you too. And as soon as the weather is a bit better, you must come to Brindleford for a break.'

'Ooh I will. Those country walks sound so relaxing.'

'And there is the most amazing bakery,' I tell her. 'With pistachio cream-filled buns the size of boulders.'

'Now you have really sold it to me.'

'Did you have a nice catch-up?' asks Nathan, when I return home.

We drove up this morning to enjoy a long weekend at the apartment, as we often do.

'It was wonderful.' I turn to him, and he kisses me.

'What did you get up to?' I ask, as I hang my coat on a stand.

'I had a lovely look around the National Gallery actually,' he tells me. 'It was very interesting. There is a top-class restaurant there too; we should book a table when the boys come.'

'Sounds good.'

I have shown Nathan around London on our previous visits, and next month we will meet his boys here and spend the weekend with them.

'So, what do you fancy doing this evening?' he asks as we glance at the twinkling lights across the city. 'Fancy a bottle of wine and a film?'

'Perfect,' I tell him, realising that it doesn't matter where you are in the world, if you are with the right person.

Home is where the heart is, after all.

A LETTER FROM SUE ROBERTS

Dear reader,

I want to say a huge thank you for choosing to read *Home This Christmas*. If you did enjoy it, and want to keep up to date with all my latest releases, just sign up at the following link. Your email address will never be shared and you can unsubscribe at any time.

www.bookouture.com/sue-roberts

I hope you loved *Home This Christmas*, and if you did I would be very grateful if you could write a review. I'd love to hear what you think, and it makes such a difference helping new readers to discover one of my books for the first time. Positive reviews really can influence readers when choosing a book!

I love hearing from my readers – you can get in touch through social media.

Thanks,

Sue Roberts

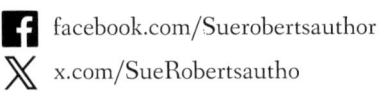 facebook.com/Suerobertsauthor
x.com/SueRobertsautho

ACKNOWLEDGEMENTS

Thank you to my fabulous publisher Bookouture and all the incredible staff involved in bringing this book to the reader. As always, a special mention goes to my wonderful editor Natalie Edwards!

Christmas is one of my favourite times of the year, and as the weather changes, I love to curl up with a good book or watch a Christmas movie. It brings back so many childhood memories, as I am sure it does for many people.

We live in such a fast-paced world, it was so nice to escape to the tranquillity of a Yorkshire village, albeit a fictional one! All those village descriptions might just have inspired me to take a trip to the Skipton Christmas market this year.

Thank you to my grown-up daughters, Rachel and Vicki, who often recall Christmas times gone by with fondness and lots of memories and funny stories. We like nothing more than getting together around the table on Christmas day.

I was thrilled to set this book in North Yorkshire, an area I have visited on many occasions, and always thoroughly enjoy. Shout out to the friendly people of Yorkshire!

Finally, a huge thanks to all of you readers and bloggers. What would we authors do without you? It means the world when you enjoy one of my books and reach out. Leaving an Amazon review is also, greatly appreciated. I hope you all have a wonderful Christmas!

PUBLISHING TEAM

Turning a manuscript into a book requires the efforts of many people. The publishing team at Bookouture would like to acknowledge everyone who contributed to this publication.

Commercial
Lauren Morrissette
Hannah Richmond
Imogen Allport

Cover design
Debbie Clement

Data and analysis
Mark Alder
Mohamed Bussuri

Editorial
Natalie Edwards
Melissa Tran

Copyeditor
Natasha Hodgson

Proofreader
Becca Allen

RAISING READERS
Books Build Bright Futures

Dear Reader,

We'd love your attention for one more page to tell you about the crisis in children's reading, and what we can all do.

Studies have shown that reading for fun is the **single biggest predictor of a child's future life chances** – more than family circumstance, parents' educational background or income. It improves academic results, mental health, wealth, communication skills, ambition and happiness.

The number of children reading for fun is in rapid decline. Young people have a lot of competition for their time, and a worryingly high number do not have a single book at home.

Hachette works extensively with schools, libraries and literacy charities, but here are some ways we can all raise more readers:

- Reading to children for just 10 minutes a day makes a difference
- Don't give up if children aren't regular readers – there will be books for them!

- Visit bookshops and libraries to get recommendations
- Encourage them to listen to audiobooks
- Support school libraries
- Give books as gifts

There's a lot more information about how to encourage children to read on our websites: **www.RaisingReaders.co.uk** and **www.JoinRaisingReaders.com**.

Thank you for reading.

Printed in Dunstable, United Kingdom

74401199R00150